D1206387

girls

girls

A PAEAN

NIC KELMAN

LITTLE, BROWN AND COMPANY
BOSTON NEW YORK LONDON

FIRST EDITION

THE CHARACTERS AND EVENTS IN THIS BOOK ARE FICTITIOUS. ANY SIMILARITY TO REAL PERSONS, LIVING OR DEAD, IS COINCIDENTAL AND NOT INTENDED BY THE AUTHOR.

LIBRARY OF CONGRESS CATALOGING-IN-PUBLICATION DATA

KELMAN, NIC.

GIRLS : A PAEAN / NIC KELMAN. — 1ST ED.

P. CM.

ISBN 0-316-71153-5

1. SEX AND SOCIETY — FICTION. 2. YOUNG WOMEN — FICTION. I. TITLE.

PS3611.E46G57 2003

813'.6 — DC21 2003047542

10 9 8 7 6 5 4 3 2 1

Q-FF

BOOK DESIGN BY IRIS WEINSTEIN

PRINTED IN THE UNITED STATES OF AMERICA

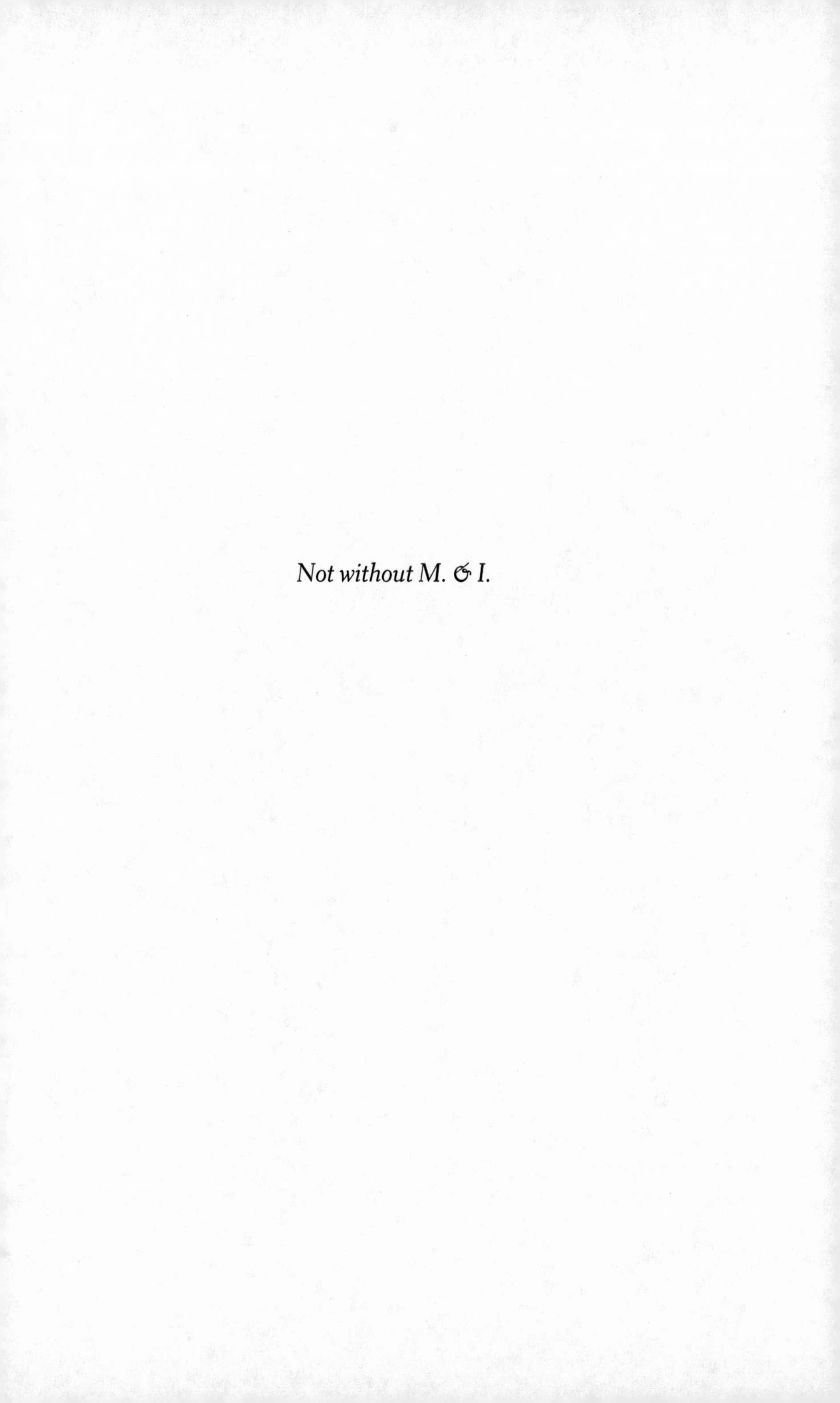

Not without M. & I.

girls

. . . lacrimae volvuntur inanes.

. . . the tears roll on, useless.

— *The Aeneid*, Virgil

What's your name?
Who's your daddy?
Is he rich like me?
Has he taken any time
To show you what you need to live?

— "Time of the Season," The Zombies

Homer. From the Greek *Hómêros:*
"He who joins the song together."

How did they get so young? These girls that only yesterday seemed so far away from us, these girls that seemed like another country. Tell me, when did they become children?

Children we want to indulge, to spoil. Children we will give anything to, everything. Except ourselves. Because, like a child, that is not something they desire. Like children, that is not something they will understand.

Yet unlike children, they make us tremble. Unlike children they can obliterate us with a glance. Just a glance. Or with their skin stretched so taut over every part of their body. With their flat bellies and unsupported breasts and bony ankles. With their, it must be said, "budding" lips because nothing is so much like a bud as the lips of a young girl, not even the buds themselves.

And when too did they cease to ignore us? When did they begin to fawn over us? When did we begin to fascinate them?

With our money and companies and perceived security. When did we become the men that made us so jealous?

Perhaps you too will see her again. Perhaps on an ice field before a medieval stone church. Perhaps crossing a small piazza, empty but for you and her and a street vendor selling wet slices of coconut. Perhaps on a crowded subway, the stench of sweat and french fries and metal forcing you both to breathe through your mouths, to pant like animals. But not as you once did.

And it will be her that will recognize you, not you her. She will say your name with hesitation and a question mark. And you will continue to look at her dumbly for one more instant as you have been for minutes and then think, "No, it can't be!" Yet you will say her name with pleasure. But not as you once did.

"My God," she'll say, "you've hardly changed!"

"And you look terrific too," you'll say. But that's not what you'll be thinking. You'll be thinking how you never would have recognized her.

She doesn't look bad, she's only — what? — in her thirties after all. For her age, in fact, she looks excellent. If there are other men you will notice then how they are staring at her. If you are on a beach you will wonder then how, if the information was correct, after three children, she still manages to wear a bikini convincingly.

And yet you still never would have recognized her.

"Is that Chanel you're wearing?" you will find yourself saying eventually, unable to stop, "I thought you hated Chanel — you always used to say it was . . . what was it?" and here you will find yourself pausing, then, as you actually say the word, smiling, openly mocking, the way you felt but never would have revealed when she used that same word so freely, so seriously, so long ago, "Bourgeois?"

"I don't know," she'll say, shrugging, "I like it now." And she will be embarrassed that you mentioned how she used to use that word. How she used to believe it meant something. Embarrassed. Even she recognizes she is not the same. But she believes it is because of something she has gained, not something she has lost.

You were in Pusan.

When you flew in, the port was hidden by cloud. You couldn't see the city at all, only the tops of mountains. The man to the right of you, a Korean, said, "Ha! That's smog. Smog! Not so pretty now, huh? Smog! Ha-ha! Ha-ha! Smog!" He went on laughing to himself as he picked up his paper again and read some more. You were still working for that investment bank, were there to find out why a container ship was behind schedule. You had been told it would probably be necessary to make an example of someone, that you should determine who.

And when you landed, it was drizzling, grey. The whole city was grey. Built of concrete and iron, built for building. You couldn't see very far down the streets in that rain that was almost a mist. Through the haze the odd red or green punched — neons, traffic lights, trash-can fires. But that was all. On the way from the airport to the hotel and the next morning from the hotel to the office, you became completely disoriented. You tried to follow your route on the map your girlfriend had given you but it was useless. You didn't know where you were.

At the office you spent a day going over the numbers, over the tonnage of materials brought in, over the daily costs of delay, over the percentage of the ship complete. The day after that you visited the ship itself. The fog had not cleared and when you stood near the command tower, you could not see the end of that unfinished deck. About halfway down it dissolved into a skeleton of girders which then itself dissolved into the mist. As if the mist were acid, as if the mist had halted construction.

And when you took the man off the job he yelled in Korean. In front of everyone he yelled at you in Korean. His face turned red, he was stocky, his stomach bulged against his belt, he threw back his shoulders, pointed his finger.

And you grew furious at him because he did not understand. This had nothing to do with him. Did he think he was playing a game here, that some conception of fairness applied? You picked up a phone to call security but he stormed out of the room. As you opened your mouth to say something to the others in the room, something about not caring, he opened the door again, yelled one last thing, and was gone. You remember thinking how puffy he looked as he stuck his torso through that gap, how the arms of his glasses splayed outwards as they ran back to his ears, remember wondering if it was the salty Korean diet that made him that way. It was only natural. You hadn't understood a word he had said.

But when you left the building, when you got in that black car that somehow ferried you from the office to the hotel in Haeundae Beach, you noticed you were shaking.

And as you shaved before dinner, looked in the mirror, you grew angry at him again, angry at him for making you feel that way, for making you feel ashamed that you did not feel ashamed. "I mean, what the fuck does he think?" you said, waving your wet razor at your own face, half-hidden in lather. "He can have the benefits without the liability?" "Screw him," you said.

The local office people took you to a vegetarian restaurant. "I don't really like vegetarian," you said but the meal was actually quite satisfying. Everything was fried and you had a lot of soju.

And when you got back to the hotel, the carpet outside your room was wet.

You had no way of knowing it was because he had been there. No way of knowing he had been too ashamed to go home to his wife and so had wandered in the rain for hours before finally sitting outside your door hoping to appeal to you. No way of knowing he had only just given up, only just decided that what he was doing was ridiculous, only just taken the stairs down as you took the elevator up. You fumbled with the card lock momentarily. As you closed the door behind you, the smell of the wet carpet was overpowering.

You are in Pusan.

You sit on the edge of your bed, drunk. You want to lie down but you can't, you feel sick when you do. Somehow your eyes find the clock. It is only 10 P.M., your girlfriend will just be getting in to work. She is a graphic designer. You pick up the phone, you call her on the company calling card.

"Hey babe!" she says, happy to hear from you. "So how is it? How's it going?"

You open your mouth but you don't know what to say. You think you may want absolution so you tell her what happened today, leaving out the part about the wet carpet, the part you don't know. But when she gives it to you, tells you you did what you had to do, you realize that wasn't it at all. You didn't want her to tell you you did the right thing, you didn't care if she thought you did the right thing or not because you already knew you did, you just wanted her to say, "I know what that's like."

But of course, she can't say that, will never say that. And if she ever could then you could no longer be with her. Then you would both be tired. Then she would be a better friend, but a worse lover.

You haven't been listening to what she's been saying. You have been thinking. But as you open your mouth to say, "Listen, do you think I should be doing something else? Something I enjoyed a little more?" you decipher the sounds she has been making.

She has been telling you how she finally used that spa certificate you gave her for her birthday, the one you could afford to buy because last year's bonus was so huge it paid off your college debt. She has been telling you how she went there for the full day and how they pampered her and how they rejuvenated her and how she felt so good afterwards, like a new woman afterwards.

There is a pause. She says, "Were you about to say something?"

"No," you say, trying to sound surprised.

"Oh," she says, "it sounded like you were about to say something." And you wonder how that could be because you're certain you didn't make any sound at all.

"Anyway, listen, babe," she continues, "I have to go — I have a meeting — but when you get back Mommy will make baby feel all better — she pwomises, OK?"

"OK," you say, chuckling. But you don't feel any better after you hang up. Just like you didn't need her to tell you you did the right thing, you also didn't need that. Mommies are for sick little boys. You aren't sick, you aren't a little boy, you don't need sympathy. There is nothing tender loving care could do for you right now, right now there is nothing even your real mother could do to make you feel better. She wouldn't, couldn't, understand what it was like any more than your girlfriend.

The headspin subsiding but not gone, you turn on the TV. There is a channel that shows only Go, twenty-four hours a day nothing but Go. This really is a different place. You change into a bathrobe, you flip through some channels. There is a channel that has some kind of beauty contest. You watch it for a few minutes and realize it's actually a talent competition. You try to masturbate a little but it's no good, you're not interested, it's not enough.

You turn out the lights. You get in bed. But you can't sleep. The Korean girls in the talent competition keep coming to mind, you can't get the Korean girls in the talent competition out of your head.

Then you remember the card. After he had told you he was sending you to Pusan, after he had told you it might be necessary to make an example of someone, your boss had looked around, had made sure there were no female employees nearby, and had said, ". . . and if you get bored, they have the best fucking hookers in all of Korea there." Then he had taken out one of his business cards and written a name on the back, the name of the concierge at the hotel to ask for, the one who'd "take care of you." "Come on, Saswat," you'd said, "you know I have a girlfriend!" "Yeah," he said, "I know," and tucked the card in your breast pocket.

You turn on the light again. Naked, you find the suit and pull out the card. You sit on the edge of the bed turning it over and over with your fingertips. You study the printed name of your boss and the Korean name written on the other side, written with a $1,200 pen. So many things run through your head. It's not really any different than masturbating, is it? I wouldn't tell her I jerked off, would I? At last you decide you'll call down and see how much it costs. Just out of curiosity.

And you can't believe how cheap it is. The high end is less than a first-class dinner in Manhattan. Now you remind yourself you could send her away. You could just see what she looks like and if you change your mind, you could just send her away. You'd have to pay her, of course, but so what, you can afford it. The Korean girls in the talent competition flash through your mind again. You tell him to send up the best thing they have. You use that word, "best."

You turn the light off. You lie on the bed. You get up and turn another light on, a less intense one, one that you imagine provides a romantic glow. You put on a robe, take a breath mint. You look around the room and realize it's a mess. In a panic because she might arrive any second, you tidy up. You throw your socks in the closet, make the bed, straighten your papers and laptop on the desk. You want her to like you, to see that you're not one of those guys, that this is — will be — something special for her. Something unique. You don't want her to think you're an animal.

There is a knock at the door, a gentle little rap at the door.

When you open it, it's not what you were expecting at all. You were expecting a Penthouse Pet, a tall woman, young but not very young, heavily made up, fake eyelashes, hair thinned from treatments, fit and sexy but with a hard, worn look, with breasts that do not sag but that do hang down enough for there to be a thin line of shadow beneath them against her ribs, with long, shapely legs that are hard and have good muscle tone but the beginnings of which, from behind, can no longer be said to be clearly distinct, with a taut stomach furrowed by two lines of muscle down its center but that still bulges slightly outwards below the line of her hips, with her skin still tight over her neck and jaw but that seems more pulled that way than pushed and is still somehow loose enough to no longer be able to follow precisely the dips and rises of the tendons in her throat. In short, someone you would want to fuck.

Instead the girl before you is not very tall nor heavily made up. Her breasts are small and natural but still find the strength to resist against the ribbed tube top she wears. It doesn't seem like she has ever exercised yet her exposed stomach is completely flat, is lean, is smooth — above it the gentle inverse V of her rib cage disappears into her top leaving a tiny shadow where the material bridges; at its bottom corners, just before it is channeled into her low-slung skirt by her hips, the bones of her pelvis form two small bumps. The curves of her legs are newly formed, have only recently grown upon the bone, are not yet done growing, have not yet begun to die. Her black hair is fine and thick and lustrous and healthy. There is a white band of reflected light across it on one side. You had forgotten what healthy hair looked like. Around her large, Eurasian eyes and small mouth, on her brow, you can't see a single wrinkle. Not one. Her skin closely follows the line of her jaw and then suddenly angles down where it meets her throat, flows into three cords on either side of her neck, one reaching for her shoulder, one touching the middle of her collarbone, one touching its end, forming the hollow that her larynx grows up out of, back towards her jaw. And her smell, her smell utterly obliterates that of the still damp carpet. Her smell is the only smell in the world.

Her whole body still strives outwards, her lips, her breasts, her thighs, her whole body has not yet decided to stop, to petrify, to crumble. You have never seen anything so ripe in all your life. That is the word that comes to mind, "ripe."

You are surprised. This is not what you expected. You desire her more than what you expected, certainly, but before the blood begins pounding in your head, you crush your desire down, push it down and away in a little box. This girl can't be more than sixteen, this girl is illegal. Illegal, that's what makes you control your desire. Not "wrong," "illegal." Your eyes flicker over her collarbone, you find yourself thinking how the hollows above it would cup sweat.

But you find yourself saying, "I think there's been a mistake. Do you understand, 'mistake'? There's been a 'mistake'?"

"I speak English," she says without an accent, without being able to help rolling her eyes slightly.

"Oh," you say. "Well, I think there's been a mistake — I asked for something else."

She shrugs her shoulders. "Fine," she says. "They can send up someone else. No problem." Without another look at you, she turns and heads off down the corridor. You watch her go, notice how tiny her ass is, how even through her skirt the dimples on either side of it are visible, how the material seems to be draped over bobbing stone. As she walks towards the elevator she begins to play some game with the pattern on the rug, stepping on only certain colors, avoiding others, almost toppling herself.

You are shaking. She is so close to being yours. This isn't

some Catholic schoolgirl on a bus, this isn't some girl to look at and think, "Damn, if only that were legal," and shake your head and not give it a second thought because it is illegal and you don't want to take the risk and what would you, could you, do anyway — you are in public. This is a hooker. This time, in this case, you only need to say the word and she can be yours. You could have your hands on her body, your mouth on the back of her neck, on her nipples, your cock inside her as her inner thighs rubbed against your pelvis, as her hands pressed down on your chest, as her upper arms squeezed her firm little breasts together, as she tossed her hair to one side of her head and looked down into your eyes and said with that tiny, pert little mouth in her accentless English, "That's it. Fuck me." You look up and down the hall. It is empty. "Wait a minute," you call out. And without a pause, without a lost step, she turns and walks back to your room and walks through your door without even looking at you. You find yourself thinking, "This probably isn't even illegal here anyway — the age of consent here is probably fifteen or sixteen — she could even be seventeen or eighteen." And you close the door behind you.

You want to devour her. You can't get enough of her in your mouth — her neck, her arms, her belly. You could eat her pussy for hours. With your girlfriend you always did it out of fairness. She went down on you so you went down on her or you wanted her to go down on you so you went down on her. You don't mind it — you know some guys who don't like to do it but do it anyway for the same reason you do — no, you don't mind it, but it never turned you on like this. All you can think about is having her in your mouth. You make her lie back on the bed, spread her arms out on the bed, and just let you pull her pussy to your mouth. Beneath your hands, the skin on her thighs is so smooth it makes you think of fax paper. You can feel the calluses on your palms scraping it as you hold her legs. You hear your stubble scratch against her right leg. Worried you might hurt her, you push her legs farther open. The tendons on her inner thighs flex out like little steel cables and where they end, where they push out the farthest forming little cups of skin above and below, the mound of her pussy drops down towards her ass. She has shaved herself completely bare, you hope that's what she's done, and the slit between her legs is so delicate it looks like someone has cut her with a scalpel. Carefully, gently, you pull the slit open with your fingertips revealing the folds of tan flesh inside. You never noticed how clumsy your fingers were before, how enormous, how ugly. Like a gorilla's, you find yourself thinking. You look at her spread open like that for a second, like a sea creature, like an anemone in that moment it reaches out to swallow a fish, and then you glance up her body. She isn't moving, she stares at the ceiling, you can't see her face. Then you put your mouth on her. For a second you are relieved to feel the odd piece of stubble pricking your lips. For a second you wonder if your girlfriend would shave herself like this. And then you are lost.

Suddenly she taps you on the shoulder, taps you on the shoulder as if you were in a line for a bus and she needed information. You look up at her, one of your ape fingers still inside her. And she says, "If you want to fuck me you should do it now — you only have fifteen minutes left." You can't believe it. You can't believe you have been doing what you have been doing for forty-five minutes. You feel like you have only just begun. And you find yourself wondering how she has been keeping track of time.

You don't really want to stop what you've been doing but you feel that you should, that you didn't pay to make her feel good, that you should get what you actually paid for. You only have to make a slight motion towards flipping her over and she is immediately on her hands and knees, thrusting her shoulder blades and her ass in the air, keeping her belly low. As you go to put yourself inside her from behind, you follow the curved groove of her sunken spine with your eyes down to the small of her back where it ends in a tiny, flat V of skin rising up like an arrowhead, its sides carved out by the two hemispheres that began sloping up at her hips, its point the beginning of the cleft of her ass — small, round, taut as a balloon — and again you are overcome by the urge to put her in your mouth. Without realizing what you are doing you find yourself licking her asshole. Tomorrow, on the plane, as you think back over the experience, as you try to reconstruct every detail, you will suddenly remember your body did this, and you will wonder where you were when it happened. There and then, on the plane, as the stewardess asks you if you want beef or chicken, the thought of it will make you ill. But here and now, in your hotel room, this thing you would never do makes you want to cum. You push yourself inside her, grab her waist with your hands, your hands that almost encompass her waist in their grip, and thrust in and out of her. The tip of your cock pushes against the roof of her uterus and every time it does she lets out a little squeal. You can't tell if it's from pain or pleasure but you think it's probably both. You worry a little bit about breaking her, about crushing her rib cage as you squeeze her little breasts that feel as firm as oranges, about snapping her arm as you pull her back onto you, about suffocating her when — after just five or six strokes — you cum and collapse on top of her.

But she is fine. She lets you lie on top of her for a second, carefully pulls you out of her making sure the condom stays in place, wipes her hand on the sheets, and squirms out from under you. You cannot move. You watch her dress. She disappears into the bathroom for a minute to fix her hair and makeup but it doesn't take long and when she is done, when you still haven't moved, she says, "I have to go."

You pull yourself up from the bed, out from under the enormous weight crushing you to the bed, and, in a daze, give her her cash. It's less than a quarter of what you had in your wallet for just one day's expenses.

She takes it without ceremony and puts it in her purse. You are still naked. At the door, after she's opened it a crack, she turns and says, "I'm sorry I reminded you about time — they always do what you did and forget about time and then get mad when they find out time is gone."

"Oh don't worry about it!" you say congenially, you say

wanting her to know you're not the same as the other men, that you'd never get mad. She just nods and says, "If you want me again, ask for Jin," and is gone.

When you get back in bed you wish you felt worse about this. You wish you felt terrible, in fact. But you don't. Instead you feel fucking fantastic. Reborn. Your head is clear, you can actually feel the sheets touching your entire body.

As you drift off to sleep you realize the concierge hadn't misunderstood, hadn't made a mistake at all. This must have been what Saswat was talking about. The best fucking hookers. The two older men simply knew what you needed better than you knew yourself.

The next day you buy your girlfriend a gift before you leave, an antique necklace. You were going to get her something anyway, you just spend a little more than you had originally planned.

You were in Pusan.

The example worked. The ship was finished on time. You saved 25 million dollars. You were a hero. The ship's cartel took you and your boss out to a restaurant that overlooked the entire city. At one point, as they served the nine dozen Wellfleet oysters, Saswat leaned over and said quietly in your ear, "Welcome to the club." You had been thinking about the man you fired, about whether he would ever eat in a restaurant like this, drink wine like this wine, but when Saswat said that, you stopped feeling guilty, alone. You at last felt like you had a companion, someone who understood.

It was a clear night. Afterwards they took you to a loud strip club, sent you to the Champagne Room with a girl named something-andy. The next morning you had a vague memory of her blowing you there, but you couldn't be certain, you were very drunk. And as you lay there that Saturday morning, your girlfriend's arm draped over your chest, the sunlight diffused over both of you by the curtains, as you lay there you thought about the last time you were that drunk, about Jin standing there outside your door, about how she looked standing there outside your door, about how she smelled standing there outside your door, how there was no other smell there, no other smell at all.

"Sing, goddess, the anger of Peleus' son Achilleus and its devastation, which put pains thousandfold upon the Achaians . . ." — *Iliad* 1:1

It is late. You are in a town in the middle of nowhere. You had managed to find a day to fly out here by yourself, to get away from everything and everyone you know and rent a truck and take a look at an enormous piece of land that happened to be for sale. You want a ranch. Somewhere no one can bother you. Somewhere with no data lines of any kind. Somewhere you can shoot anyone you didn't invite.

And afterwards, once the sun had gone down, you had driven the thirty or so miles to the nearest town to get some dinner. For the first time in about seventeen years you don't know where you'll be staying the night and you are surprised how good that feels. It's something you never would have thought could make you feel anything but anxious.

So you park at the only restaurant in town, a diner with rigs parked nearby. It's not a truck stop per se, just one of those places truckers stop because there's nowhere else.

You sit down in a booth and the waitress brings you a menu. She doesn't say anything to you, doesn't even give you a second look. And you are surprised how much it irritates you to be treated like that, like anyone else. It's something you thought would never make you feel anything but relaxed.

And as you are looking at the menu you catch the door open out of the corner of your eye and the person who comes in walks right up next to you and says, "Excuse me."

You look up. Standing there is a large man, much larger than you, wearing a grimy T-shirt and blue jeans and a belt buckle that says ALLIE'S GATOR FARM. His worn black baseball cap says CATERPILLAR in yellow letters and you are suddenly very aware that yours is not only new but says ALPHAGENESIS.

"Yes?" you say.

"You're in my booth," the man says. He's not picking a fight, just stating a fact, like you've made a genuine mistake, like you stopped to ask him directions and he's telling you you took a wrong turn.

"Oh," you say. "Well I don't mind if we share, that's no problem," you say with the friendly smile that has closed more deals than you can remember. Well, unless you actually try to remember.

He looks over at the empty side of the booth and then looks back at you and says, "No, I don't think so. I think I'd like my booth to myself just right now." And again he looks at you without hostility. He's simply telling you what you need to know.

You look around the diner. You know where this would have to go from here. So you don't say anything more. You just get up and, with no other booths free, start to walk over to the counter. But he says, "Hey!" as you walk away.

And this time when you turn around you're ready to take a stand right there in your new sneakers. This has gone far enough, you think, I don't care what happens, you think, I'm not going to let this redneck push me around anymore.

But he's holding your coat out to you. "You forgot your coat," he says.

"Thanks," you say, taking it from him.

"No problem," he says, sinking into your booth. "What is that anyway? Calf? It's nice, real soft."

"No," you say, "I think it's sheep."

"Huh," he says picking up his menu, "I didn't know they could make sheep that soft."

As you sit down at the counter, sit down on one of the metal stools with their worn-out padding, and pick up a menu, you hear the waitress go up to him behind you and say, "Hey, Jake, how you doing? Usual?" and the reply, "Howdy, Lu-Ann, yes please, if you don't mind."

And as you eat your third-rate chicken-fried steak it occurs to you that the way you feel has nothing to do with your job or with all the responsibilities you have made for yourself outside your job. You realize that the way you feel will never go away. You realize that, as long as you are around other men, it can never stop.

There are certain mammals that have a little hook at the end of their penis. Their couplings are so violent they could never copulate successfully without it. But sometimes, when they mate, they become caught. Unable to separate they cannot forage or sleep or run. And so they die like that. Joined.

I remember holding your hand in Avignon.

We walked through the medieval streets, close like canyons, twisting our ankles on the cobblestones. The sun was orange, yellow, made everything beautiful, the laundry strung from window to window, the stray dogs pissing in the gutters.

We had always talked about going there when we were in college. You had done your thesis on the papal period, wanted to see all the places that were so important, the places that had only been words and silver halides to you. This was a dream come true for you.

At that palace like a fortress, like some vampire's hall, you told me what happened here, who was killed there. On the walls, from where we could see the collapsed bridge, you sang the song. Your French was perfect. A little English girl was there and when she heard you singing, she ran away from her mother and asked you if you could teach her the song. You held her tiny hands while you listened to her, took her request as seriously as she did, laughed and looked at me when she was done asking. The wind blew your hair into your face but I think you saw me smile. You taught her the song and her mother thanked you as if you had done her the greatest favor, endured the greatest injustice.

We stayed in a suite at the Louis XIV. The night we arrived there was champagne waiting for us in the room. I had asked for it. The night we arrived you tried to pour it down your naked breast into my open mouth, but instead of cascading off your nipple, the stream split there, clung to the underside of your breast, ran down your body to where it touched the bed. I licked up what I could as it flowed but it made the mattress wet anyway.

I bought you everything you wanted. Everything. The Crusader's cross hammered out in silver, inlaid with onyx. The Regency armoire that cost as much to ship back as to buy. A letter of excommunication signed by Pope Innocent VI.

But you said you didn't want the bracelet. You looked at it very closely but then stood upright and said, "No, I don't really want it." You didn't know I saw you touch the glass bangle you were wearing as you spoke, the bangle I had brought you back from a business trip to London. You probably didn't know you touched it yourself.

You seemed so happy. I enjoyed your company so much. I wasn't particularly interested in the medieval history of the papacy but it made you so excited, made you come so much alive, that I could listen to you talk about it for hours. Your eyes lit up when you talked about it, shone, not like when you talked about your work at the PR firm. I remembered why I'd taken you so far to ask you a question I already knew the answer to.

The last night there, after dinner, near a lead fountain in the middle of a crossroads, I asked you to marry me. You said yes, of course. And that was what was supposed to happen. There was nothing wrong, nothing wrong at all. I felt fine.

On the flight back you looked at the ring every so often, hoped the woman next to you would say how pretty it was, ask you about it. But she was much older, she read and she ate and she said nothing. At last, somewhere over the middle of the Atlantic Ocean, you put your arms around my neck and sighed and closed your eyes and said, "It's like a fairy tale." I kissed your brow and moved your left arm a little so I could see the report I was trying to read.

But I do remember holding your hand in Avignon.

"'To me you are the most hateful of all the kings the gods love. Forever quarrelling is dear to your heart, and wars and

battles; and if you are very strong indeed, that is a god's gift.'"
— Agamemnon to Achilles, *Iliad* 1:176

You wake in the night sometimes, your heart pounding with that fear, that terror that you are not secure, that you are exposed, that for all your money and servants and employees, tomorrow you may be out on the street — working in a factory, driving a bus — fighting with a woman as old as you are about whether or not you can afford to see a movie. Just a lousy movie. You lie there and stare at where the ceiling would be in the dark and you realize that there is someone next to you. But you don't know who. You weren't even that drunk. There were, as always, several candidates — temps, struggling actresses, younger sisters. They couldn't wait to talk to you, to listen to you, to find you fascinating. And now one of them lies next to you. Half your age, you know that, she must be. But that is all you know. Her face, her name, her body are gone.

And you hate yourself for being weak, for taking the drug again, for smoking the cigarette you had forborne. You wish she wasn't there, whoever she is.

In the morning, you wake and she is in your shower. You wonder what she looks like but it doesn't matter, no matter what she looks like she must go. But then the shower is turned off and she steps into your room, drying her whole body with a hand towel, unashamed of her nakedness. Not like the women you know your own age, that can't wait to hide their sagging flesh, turn off lights, wear long skirts. And her wet hair and the glistening of her nipples in the morning sun and her anklet or her tattoo or her pierced tongue or whatever it is makes you shiver and you know you will not tell her to leave, that you will listen to her babble over lunch and nod and smile. But not because you are trying to please her. Because watching her really does make you smile, indulging her really does make you happy for a moment. Watching something free, unweighted, like setting a dog loose on a beach. You are too tired to run like that, too anxious to enjoy the sun and the waves, but seeing the animal relax, take pleasure, at least helps you remember what it was like. In the earning of things you have lost the ability to enjoy them. And others can only enjoy them because they did not earn them.

If you are running with a friend and the two of you can have a conversation as you're running, you can be sure you're not getting anything out of the run.

You will let her dress you, let her teach you new dances, take you to new clubs, new bars, because even though you know it does not really matter, it matters to her. You will let her take you to a dirty Thai restaurant that has mediocre food and when she says, "How is it?" you will say, "Great," and she'll say, "I told you!" and you'll leave it at that because you can't explain and you'd rather she was happy and ignorant than informed and miserable. In fact it is because of this very quality that you are drawn to her and those like her and why you can never be with one too long. Because then they become like you, when they become informed, they become tired like you, jaded. But when they still do not yet understand the world, they can still remind you of joy. They are little bundles of joy, they are. You can live your life through them even though you are dead. These little bundles of joy in string bikinis who are not too tired to go parasailing, still thrilled at the prospect of skydiving, who have not yet discovered that there is nothing worth discovering. You want to possess them, yes. But like a spirit, not an owner.

"'Even as Phoibos Apollo is taking away my Chryseis . . . I shall take the fair-cheeked Briseis, your prize . . . that you may learn well how much greater I am than you . . .'" — Agamemnon to Achilles, *Iliad* 1:182

We smile when they tell us we don't know anything and that we understand even less.

Smile when they berate us for being boring, for wanting nothing more than to sit still when we have a moment in which we do not need to work, despite the money and the toys we have, the money and the toys we always dreamed of. "We could do anything," they say. "Fly to China for the weekend, race cars, anything, and all you want to do is sit there and watch the largest television I've ever seen." Yes that is all we want but not all we wanted. The energy is gone for all else, gone, and they should be thankful for that because that is why we need them, that is why they make us tremble, that is why we smile at them and say nothing, because they are our energy now, they have the energy we have spent elsewhere, we need them to get us up off the couch because without them, a moment's peace would be enough.

Smile, find it charming when they're impressed by what used to impress us — champagne, private jets, expensive cigarettes — again, we need them for that. Without them we have done all this for nothing.

What did even the gods themselves prize above all other sacrifices?

What was the only thing that even they could take only once?

You always asked me those questions. Before we knew we were getting divorced, before you opened the note from Daniel's daughter, before your friend saw me in Seattle with that undergraduate that had attended my lecture. You asked me one of those questions on our very first date. “God, those things are so fake! I think that’s so unattractive, don’t you?” you asked.

Even if you had put it differently, I would have known the answer. Your small cup and push-up bra told me what you wanted me to say. “Oh, absolutely,” I said even though I liked the waitress’s breasts. Did you need to ask me that? Saying nothing at all would have been better. Then I never would have been forced to put the lie into words, then at least some kind of ambiguity would have remained.

Yet those early ones were always easy. I knew what to say if you asked me if you looked fat, if a skirt looked good, if you could get away with those boots. But the longer we knew each other, the more times we had sex, the more and more difficult they grew.

There was the phase you went through when you made a point of staring at other men when I was talking to you. It made you so angry when I looked at other women you thought you’d show me what it was like. But when I didn’t react, you became even more furious. “Why don’t you care? If you loved me, you’d care,” you yelled at me. That was the first question I didn’t know how to answer. I didn’t understand why it wouldn’t be possible for me to love you and trust you.

But there were many more after that, many more questions I didn’t know how to answer, questions you always asked me after sex, questions that had obviously been poisoning your mind for days, for weeks. Questions like, “If I brought another girl home with me, would you sleep with her?” Questions like, “If I was kidnapped, how long would you wait before you slept with someone else?" Questions like, "How much do you love me?"

After the first one, after I said, "Well I guess if you brought her home with you I would," after you refused to return my calls for a week, I learned very quickly what I was supposed to do if I wanted you to stay with me. I learned very quickly that even when I kept no secrets from you, you still didn't want to hear the truth.

Where did those questions come from? From fears or expectations or both or something else entirely? Why did you ask me those questions if you didn't want to hear the answers? Why did you teach me to lie to you?

In Turkish the term is *chitter-chitter*, which means "freshly baked," "ready to eat." In Japanese, *hatsuikuzakari no bi*, meaning "the blossoming beauty of a girl in the midst of developing." In Afrikaans, *hoë ouderdom*, which means "the riper, the better." In Seri Indian it is *ziix cöima*, which translates as "body that has happened," *ziix* being otherwise used primarily to refer to corpses or "bodies that are no longer happening." In Urdu it is . . .

It is somebody's birthday, you're not sure whose. Maybe the fat blonde with the irritating cackle, maybe the German designer fresh out of school. You move from cab to cab and bar to bar, a swarm of cocktail-devouring bankers and consultants and IT pros. Everywhere the air is thick, visible. Now and then you find yourself wondering if the little table candles could cause it to ignite. Now and then you imagine a firestorm sterilizing the bar. You imagine this, now and then, even though you know the haze is evaporated sweat, even though you know evaporated sweat cannot catch fire.

Except tonight is not like other nights. Tonight your girlfriend is with you. You have been seeing her for some time, a few years. Perhaps more, perhaps slightly less. You think you know her quite well. You know she likes brioche. You know she claims to be better at chess than she is. You know her sense of humor is more vulgar than you'd like. You know she tells her older brother things she does not tell you. You know you find her looking in the mirror sometimes — frozen, toothbrush in hand, mouth full of foam — and when she sees you behind her she stops looking and begins to brush once more. Usually if the two of you are out and not out "on a date," she goes out with her friends and you go out with yours. But tonight all her friends are busy. So here she is, with you, asking you who people are, telling you to introduce her.

Tonight is also not like other nights because you arranged to meet an old high school friend at one of the bars. A "we should get together sometime" that somehow became specific. And sure enough, as if conjured, as if your cell phone communicated with another world, he appears at the appointed place and time.

He does not need to force his way through the crowd, it

parts before him. You never forgot he was a linebacker in high school but over the years, in your memory, he had grown smaller. It was only high school, after all. But as the people at the bar make room for him you realize that, of course, he must have continued to grow even though you were not there to see it. You wonder how he managed to get in wearing blue jeans.

"There he is," you say to your girlfriend. "Come on — I want you to meet him." The two of you excuse yourselves from the area your group has staked out, "prime real estate" as one friend would call it because you can see the front door. As your girlfriend uncrosses her legs, stands up, she watches some Italian friend of a friend. His eyes are fastened on her in turn, but below her waist.

"I do believe Paolo was just trying to see my panties," she says to you. She's very good with names, your girlfriend, even after a couple of Cosmos.

"Who's Paolo?" you ask as you begin to shove your way through the crowd, shoulder first. Dragged behind you, in your wake, she does not answer. She knows you don't really care who Paolo is.

The people at the bar make room for you after you slap your friend's broad back and he turns around. As if surrounded by a magnetic field his rotation pushes back everything around him. Out of the corner of your eye you can see your girlfriend is surprised that this was once a close friend of yours. He has a very different look from your friends now, a look less at home here than in Irish pubs with sticky floors and broken dartboards.

She stands by patiently while the two of you spread your arms wide, yell, "Heyyyyy!" and begin to shake hands. You think the better of it and draw him down to you for a hug. Your clasped hands remaining between you, the embrace is awkward.

You look at your girlfriend after you release each other, as he straightens up. Now she is expectant.

"Penny, Clay. Clay, Penny," you say as they look at each other. They shake hands.

"Nice to meet you," says Clay.

"Likewise," says Penny. She greets him as she has not greeted anyone so far. It's not that she doesn't like your friends or that she's shy. It's just that she has her friends and you have yours and that's the way she'd like it to stay. So throughout the introductions she has been reserved, if curious. But with Clay, the right corner of her mouth turns up a little; with Clay, she lowers her head slightly, causing herself to look at him with upturned eyes. "I hear you're a cop," she adds.

"That's my story and I'm sticking to it," he says with a smile. He raises his pint to her and takes a sip. She actually laughs.

"Neat," she says.

The three of you head back to the booths near the wall. You try to keep Clay as far as possible from the irritating blonde but you cannot escape her laugh. Once you get past the catching up, once Penny has gathered a satisfactory number of embarrassing stories about you, once she is familiar enough with him, her questions become bold.

"What kinds of guns have you used," she asks, "have you ever used a machine gun?" "Have you ever had to tackle anyone on the street?" "Do they really have the toilets right there in the cells?" she asks. "If they do, I could definitely never go to prison."

You consider saying something to her, whispering to her to cut it out when he talks to the waitress, goes to the men's room, but you decide not to. He doesn't seem to mind the celebrity, doesn't seem to mind being exotic. Besides, she wouldn't listen anyway.

Unable to avoid your area of expertise, you are drawn into a conversation near you, a conversation about trade-agreement trends. As you talk, you glance over at your girlfriend every now and then. You can't hear what she's saying but she's laughing a lot, touching your friend a lot, poking his stomach a lot. Even from where you're sitting, you can see her fingers meet resistance. He must have the time to work out every day. Her eyes flicker to his mouth when he talks and move over his chest, his biceps, when she thinks he isn't looking, when he reaches out for his drink or watches someone walk by. On the inside of his left arm, you notice, he has the kind of scar you cannot get from falling off a horse or a boat.

And yet you discover you are not jealous. Instead, as the mousy woman next to you drones on about the dissolution of OPEC, you find yourself imagining your girlfriend going down on him, imagining the two of them in a bathroom here, your girlfriend squatting before him, legs spread, miniskirt hiked up, one hand in her panties, the other around his cock. The last time you were here, a few months ago, just the two of you alone, she blew you there like that. The bathrooms are single occupancy and when she led you back to the bar there was a long line of surprised people for her to giggle her way past. You discover that, instead of making you jealous, their flirtation is turning you on.

The conversation over, you rejoin them. Penny is trying to explain what she does for a living. You're pretty sure Clay doesn't understand completely but you could be wrong. You seem to remember he did pretty well in school, seem to remember something about the police academy entrance exam being significantly harder than most people think it is.

You continue to talk. Sometimes other people from your group join you, say, "Really?" when you tell them what Clay does.

It gets late, people leave, your group dwindles. The blonde shrieks as she stumbles on the steps down to the street. Through the window near your booth you can see her telling everyone outside she's OK. Now none of you can remember what you were talking about only a moment ago. You and Clay take sips of your beers. With her elbows, your girlfriend leans heavily on the table, plays with a swizzle stick that was left behind. She moves the tip this way and that, studies its motion. Concentrating hard, she drags tiny pools of spilled liquid out over the glass then pushes them back together. Suddenly, before you can stop her, she looks at Clay and asks, "Have you ever killed anyone?"

You have been wondering the same thing all night yet you still say, "Penny!"

"Sorry," she says right away, "sorry. Shouldn't have asked that — it's serious, I know . . . sorry . . ."

"No, that's OK," says Clay with a shrug. But he doesn't answer.

"ooop!" says Penny. "I need the little girl's room — excuse me . . ." Not without effort she stands up to exit the semicircular booth. Instead of getting up, Clay slides as far back as he can to let her by. When she squeezes past, her ass almost touches his face. You watch him watch her find her way through the bar, through the French rap bouncing off the retro plastic chairs. You are about to say something but the waitress appears.

"Last call, guys . . . ," she says.

"Shit," says Clay. "What time is it?"

"About four," you say. "Why?" The waitress stands there looking back and forth between you.

"Sorry," Clay says to the waitress, "I think we're good, right?" He looks at you.

"Yes, thank you — we're fine — I'll close out my tab."

"OK," she says and disappears.

"What's the matter?" you ask, concerned. He is looking at a small piece of paper he has just taken out of his wallet.

"I think I missed the last train," he says.

"Oh," you say, relieved. "Don't worry about that! You can stay with us!"

"Really?" he says. "You don't mind?"

"No — not at all — don't be silly — of course! We have a guest room — it's no problem, really."

"OK," he says. "Thanks man."

"No problem," you say, raising your glass to him. "What are old friends for?"

"Hey guys, what's up?" asks your girlfriend, returned. She scoots into the booth next to Clay, perching on the end of the seat.

"Time to go," you say.

"Awww," she says pouting, looking at Clay, "I was just beginning to enjoy myself. . . ." She smiles. You haven't seen her act like this in a long time, possibly since you met. You find yourself wondering if she's like this when she's out with her friends. They're all beautiful, they must get hit on all the time. The waitress brings the check as Clay adds, "I'm staying over, I hope that's OK. . . ."

Penny glances at you as you sign the little slips of paper then looks back at your friend and answers, "Of course, don't be silly — we have a spare room."

While you hail the cab, they continue to talk. You can't hear what they're saying but as the cab pulls up you hear Penny chuckling again. "You're bad," she says as they walk over.

Clay sits up front, there isn't enough space for the three of you in back. After you give the driver your address, Penny slides up close to you and whispers, "I can't wait to get you home." She begins kissing your neck with an open mouth but no tongue, begins rubbing your cock through your pants. You can't help pinching her nipples through her thin silk blouse. You glance up every now and then to see if Clay is looking. Not that you know how you'd feel if he was, embarrassed or excited, you just know you have to look. But he never turns around. He just stares out the window, light sliding across his face, slithering over the bridge of his nose. But you still grab your girlfriend's wrist when she starts to undo your zipper.

When you open the door to your apartment, your dog is right there. He leaps up at you and Penny and then circles Clay, sniffing the cuffs of his pants before leaping up at him too. Clay squats down and rubs the scruff of the dog's neck with both hands. "What's his name?" he asks.

"He's a Pharaoh Hound," you say, "purebreed . . . his name's Romulus."

"I'll just get your room ready," Penny says, folding her shawl over a chair near the door, disappearing into the apartment.

While you wait for her, you show Clay the investments you and Penny have made together. The dog follows at your heels. Wherever you stop he sits and looks up at Clay hopefully. Clay listens without comment as you catalog the designers and painters in your house. He sits in a Corbusier when you tell him to, nods when you say, "Isn't it comfortable?" When you tell him how much you paid for the minor Pollock you picked up at auction he raises his eyebrows. "I know," you say, "can you believe it? Of course, it's not a well-cataloged piece, but still . . ." At the window, he says, "Great view." He picks up a photo from the mantel and studies it.

"That's me and Penny and Penny's parents on her dad's boat. Near Corfu, I think," you say. Nobody uses the word "yacht" anymore. In the photograph, Penny wears a bikini.

"I look so fat in that picture," she says from behind you. Clay replaces the frame.

"All set?" you ask.

"Yup," she says.

"Great," you say. "Come on, I'll show you where you're sleeping."

"This is great," he says when he sees the room, "thanks, guys."

"You're welcome," says Penny. "You know where the bathroom is. . . ."

"And the kitchen," you add, "help yourself if you want anything — mi casa es tu casa. . . ."

"Cool — great, thanks," he says again, sitting on the edge of the bed.

"Good night," you say. As you begin to close the door, the dog shoots through between your legs, squeezes into the room. You open the door again.

"Come on, Ro, get out of there, come on," you command, pointing at your feet. The dog stands in the middle of the room, stares at you blankly.

Clay looks at him and says, "It's cool, don't worry about it, I don't mind if you don't mind."

"No, I don't mind," you say. "He's allowed to sleep anywhere except our room, so . . ."

"Just don't let him up on the bed," says Penny, "he'll ruin those sheets. . . ."

"OK, no problem – good night," says Clay. The dog, somehow comprehending, curls up on the rug. Before you even close the door, Clay has his T-shirt off and is standing up to undo his pants.

In your own room, after you have both brushed your teeth, after you have both undressed, after you have hung your clothes up because they are too expensive to just toss on a chair or the floor no matter how tired you are, after Penny has put her jewelry away in its box, after you have asked her if she needs the alarm set for some reason, after you've closed the door and turned off the lights, after you both get into bed, she rolls on top of you and says, "Oh no you don't – we have a transaction to conduct, mister."

You open your eyes and look at her, tiger-striped by the orange light from the street. She slides down your body and begins sucking your cock. She knows that almost always gets you interested no matter how late it is. And sure enough, you find you begin to push your pelvis up into her face, sure enough your hands find their way to the back of her head, your fingers into her hair.

Once you are hard enough, she flips over onto her back, spreads her legs, and, while fingering herself, says, "Fuck me." She is careful to use her middle finger, she knows that also makes you want to fuck her.

And as you fuck her, she keeps her eyes closed more than usual, keeps her hands off your body, grips the headboard. You find yourself wondering if she is pretending you are someone else, wondering if she is pretending you are Clay. And suddenly you are imagining Clay fucking her. It makes you want to cum. You ask, "Who are you thinking about?"

"What do you mean?" she says. She keeps her eyes closed.

"It's OK — I don't mind, tell me." You have slowed down, almost stopped. She doesn't answer. "It's Clay, isn't it?" She opens her eyes, studies your face for a moment.

"Maybe," she says.

"Yeah?" you say, starting to fuck her again, hard but slowly. "You want him to fuck you?"

"Maybe," she says again, closing her eyes every time you push into her and then opening them again as you slide out.

"Yeah?" you say. "You think he's got a big cock?" She doesn't answer, only moans. Your thrusts are more violent now. "You want to suck his big, fat cock while I fuck you? You want him to cum in your mouth while I fuck you?" Her eyes are closed again, she is moaning.

"Yes," she says. "Yes. I want to suck his cock. . . ."

Hearing her say it almost makes you cum. Almost. Instead, before you even know what you're doing, you stop moving in and out of her body and say, "Let's do it."

She opens her eyes and looks at you for a minute. You just meet her gaze. "Really?" she asks.

"You want to?" you ask.

"I don't know," she says, a little confused. "You don't mind?"

"God no," you say. And it's true, you realize, you wouldn't mind at all. Clay is no threat to you. If it was one of your banker or lawyer friends — especially one or two in particular, the ones with the biggest accounts — then maybe you'd mind. But not Clay. You know your girlfriend would never be foolish enough to leave you for someone like him.

Suddenly conspiratorial she asks, "Do you think he'd be into it? Doesn't he have a girlfriend?"

"Of course he would — he's only been seeing her a few weeks . . . besides, no man in their right mind would turn down a chance to sleep with you." Now you are conversing, even though you are still inside her, the word "fuck" seems suddenly inappropriate.

"What should we do?" She is intrigued by the idea now, you can see it excites her.

"I don't know," you say. "Go in there — get in bed with him . . . get him interested then ask him if he minds if I join you — tell him you want both of us at once — he won't say no if he's already thinking he can have you. . . ."

"Really?" she says.

"Yeah — go on, try it — it'll work . . . ," you say, telling her to do something you would never have the balls to do yourself.

She slips out of bed and you follow her into the hall. She looks at you before she opens the door to the guest room. "Go on," you hiss. She opens the door and disappears. You stand close by and listen but you can't hear anything. You jerk off a little, imagine her sucking Clay's cock. You can't tell how much time passes. Maybe two minutes, maybe twenty. Then she opens the door and, without saying anything, turns around and walks back to the bed. Clay is sitting on the edge, naked. She pushes him back, gets on the bed herself, on all fours, and starts licking the shaft of his cock, up and down. She looks at you as she does this and you almost cum right there in the doorway, looking at your girlfriend's mouth on another man's cock. You hurry over to the bed and kneel behind her. When you push your own cock into her she is as wet as she's ever been.

After a minute or two she straightens up, bends back, slips a hand around behind your head, and pulls your ear down to her mouth.

"Can I fuck him?" she whispers.

You just nod but you think it's amusing that she asked. She obviously has no idea how much this turns you on, how much it overcomes your habituation to her. She obviously doesn't understand how watching her fuck someone else will make her stand out against the world she has long since blended into, the world you have made together, a world you know so well that, by now, you have long since lost not merely the desire, but even the need to look at it. It will be like fucking her somewhere new, somewhere you've never fucked her before — a dressing room, a rental car, a hiking trail — somewhere she can no longer hide in plain sight and where, therefore, you become capable of noticing her once more, once more become capable of seeing her body. It will be like that only better. She obviously doesn't realize that, for you, this is as exciting as fucking her for the very first time.

And when, after she has cum with you in her pussy and Clay in her mouth, after she has cum with Clay in her pussy and you in her mouth, after she has recovered from cumming with Clay in her pussy and you in her ass (screaming – yes, screaming so you worry about the upstairs neighbors for a second, just a second – screaming: "ohgodohfuckohgodOHFUCK," eyes rolled back in her head, you barely moving in case you cum yourself because the tip of Clay's cock feels like a little tongue inside your girlfriend's body, a little tongue inside your girlfriend's body sliding up and down the underside of your own cock), after that, when she tells you both to cum on her tits, all it takes is for her to wrap her hand around your cock. That's all it takes. She has to move her hand back and forth once or twice before Clay cums, but for you all she has to do is wrap her hand around your cock. Just knowing that another man is about to cum on her, that she wants another man to cum on her at the same time as you, is enough.

You wake not too long after dozing off. At least you think it's not too long, you can't really tell. You just know there isn't enough space in this one bed for all of you to be comfortable. You nudge your girlfriend, wake her too, beckon her back to your room. It doesn't occur to you to leave her sleeping there with him. Clay is snoring heavily, he doesn't stir even though by now the sunlight in the room is quite intense. As you get into your own bed you realize you are smiling, have been smiling. To have done something like this, something you feel certain none of your friends have done with their girlfriends (with hookers, yes, perhaps, but not with anyone they have a relationship with), makes you feel superior. You feel as if, of all the people you know, you are the only one who has dared to live. As you pull the covers up to your chin, you imagine you know how the Caesars must have felt.

And you sleep so soundly that, later that morning, you do not wake when your girlfriend wakes. Instead, you are asleep when she smiles at you and kisses you lightly on the forehead and gets up to go pee. You are asleep when she finds Clay standing in the bathroom, naked, washing his face, your dog at his feet. Are asleep when they look at each other and grin, sheepishly. Are asleep when she finds herself unable to avoid glancing down between his legs, when she looks up to find Clay still looking at her but no longer sheepish. Asleep when she finds herself shooing the dog, reluctant to move, out of the bathroom, finds herself making the space to kneel. Asleep when, even though she has always spit your cum out and always will, always let it dribble out over her chin by way of compensation, she not only swallows, but whimpers when the cock in her mouth ceases to pulse.

And you will be asleep when, even though only a few hours before you watched her do almost this same thing to this same man, even though she still has his dried semen encrusted on her chest like salt crystallized in the sun, even though you are quite right in thinking she will never leave you for someone like him, you will be asleep when she stands up and says quietly, "Don't tell him about this, OK?"

There is a pop music star on the covers of all the magazines. She is sixteen but she poses in cutoff shirts and plaid miniskirts hiked up to her waist as she lies on beds covered with stuffed animals. She is sixteen and has had her tits done. She is sixteen and her hit song is titled, "Give It to Me Again."

Then she says in an interview, "I wear skimpy clothes — sure — but it's only because it gets so hot onstage. I get a lot of criticism from mothers' groups about being under eighteen and building an image as a sex object — but I don't know what they're talking about, I don't try to do that."

And you have to laugh. Not just because she's lying so shamelessly but because the mothers' groups want to believe she has to try.

When your life first became not-living, when you first became undead, you tried other things, so many other things, things that could make you feel alive again or forget that you weren't, things that let you escape, things that set you free. Skydiving, bungee jumping, mountain climbing, video games, heroin. But you habituated to all of them. You had to keep opening the chute later, jumping over something sharper, increasing the rating, playing longer. With all of them you had to keep upping the dosage until there was nowhere left to go.

And maybe, just maybe, that night after the girl had left but before you fell asleep, you had an epiphany that this was not an epiphany. That this had nothing to do with Pusan, or the business card with the pimp's name, or the mist, or any of that crap. Maybe you realized that somewhere along the way you had begun to feel like this but you couldn't have said precisely where or when or how. Maybe this is, in fact, much more likely.

"'Brother by marriage to me, who am a nasty bitch evil-intriguing, how I wish that on that day when my mother first bore me the foul whirlwind of the storm had caught me away and swept me to the mountain, or into the wash of the sea deep-thundering where the waves would have swept me away before all these things had happened. Yet since the gods had brought it about that these vile things must be, I wish I had been the wife of a better man than this is, one who knew modesty and all things of shame that men say. But this man's heart is no steadfast thing, nor yet will it be so ever hereafter; for that I think he shall take the consequence. But come now, come in and rest on this chair, my brother, since it is on your heart beyond all that the hard work has fallen for the sake of dishonoured me and the blind act of Alexandros, us two, on whom Zeus set a vile destiny, so that hereafter we shall be made into things of song for the men of the future.'" — Helen, *Iliad* 6:343

You are in South Beach with some girl, somebody a friend of yours set you up with, not a hooker exactly but a party girl, a girl men like you can call when you're in town and say, "Hey, so-and-so gave me your number and said we should get together," and she'll say, "Sure, sounds like fun," and let you take her out to dinner and buy her some clothes or even some jewelry and let you fuck her.

So you're there with her and you're walking around and you buy a pretzel and a soda and then she wants to go into the Versace boutique. So you go in. And as soon as you go in, the manager comes over to you and says he's sorry but they don't allow food or drinks in the store. And the girl says, "Oh, OK, no problem — we'll just come back in a bit — come on, you can finish that on the beach and we'll come back after."

But for some reason — maybe the young manager just bothers you somehow — for some reason anyway, you say, "No — if you want to shop here now, you're going to shop here now," and you put your soda and your pretzel down on one of the leather chairs and you take out your wallet.

And the manager laughs. "Sir — please," he says.

And you say, "No, I'm serious, how much will it cost me to eat a pretzel and drink a soda in here?"

And he says, "Sir, it's a store policy." The girl shifts around, a little embarrassed, she has been in here before and would like to come again, she lives here, she smiles nervously at the sales assistant over by the counter, pushes her hair back behind her right ear with one finger.

And you say, "Fifty bucks?"

And he says, "Sir . . ."

"A hundred?" you are taking fifties out of your wallet. The girl has stopped fidgeting. The manager has stopped talking. Now he too looks nervous but he's stopped talking.

"Two hundred?"

"Fine," the manager says at last. And you hand him the money and he slips it in his pocket and you pick up your pretzel and your soda and sit down in the leather chair and say to the girl, "Well, go on — try some things on."

Over by the counter the manager gives one of your fifties to the sales assistant to keep her quiet. He probably thinks you're a fool, that you must be an idiot to spend two hundred dollars the way you just did. What he doesn't realize is that he lost out on the transaction. What he doesn't realize, may never realize, is that what you just bought was worth much more than a lousy two hundred bucks.

And afterwards, when you leave, when the girl leaves with a bag or two, she has forgotten her embarrassment and she says, "That was SO funny — you are SO cool!" And she slips her arm through yours and snuggles up to you. But you didn't think it was funny, you've never thought it was funny.

As he watched General Hooker's troops and their traveling brothel cross the river at Fredricksburg, General Lee observed: "It is well that war is so terrible or we should grow too fond of it."

But do you remember when, that first night, there was a mouse?

There were cardboard boxes of different shapes and sizes everywhere and we sat on a rug we had unrolled and ate Chinese food from the smallest cardboard boxes of all. And just as I handed you the chicken you dropped it and leapt to your feet and said, "ohmygodamouse!" Even in the dim light of the one halogen lamp we had managed to find and unpack and plug in, I could see a long dark thick stain spreading out over the rug from the dropped box of chicken.

I set the chicken upright and stood up and said, "Where?"

"Somewhere over there," you said and pointed.

"Well, we'll just get some traps in the —"

"There!" you said. "Look!"

And I looked and there was a mouse shooting across the channel between two rows of boxes, his shadow much bigger than he was. In fact I might have only seen his shadow, not the mouse himself.

"We have to get rid of it now," you said but you looked at me.

So I sighed and I said, "OK but you get to clean up that sauce — I'm glad this wasn't one of the good rugs," and I found the box you had labeled LEGS and got out a table leg and pushed some boxes around until the mouse made a break for the skirting board. But when he got to the wall it was in the middle and there was no hole and so he had to run the length of the dim empty room hugging the wall closely, his tiny claws skittering on the bare wood floor and I intercepted him in the corner, cut him off at the pass, and smashed his head in with one blow of the table leg. I was so accurate his body was completely intact, it was only his head that had become a matted clump of fur and red and one bulging black eye.

You didn't even want to look at it so when we were done eating I picked him up with my chopsticks and put him in the box of chicken where what was left of the dark, almost-black sauce swallowed him up like a tar pit and I closed the box up and threw it away with the rest of the trash. We ended up throwing the rug away too, the stain wouldn't come out.

Do you remember any of that?

"' . . . this was no lie when you spoke of my madness. I was mad, I myself will not deny it. Worth many fighters is that man whom Zeus in his heart loves, as now he has honoured this man and beaten down the Achaian people. But since I was mad, in the persuasion of my heart's evil, I am willing to make all good, and give back gifts in abundance . . . seven unfired tripods; ten talents' weight of gold . . . twelve horses, strong, race-competitors . . . [and] seven women of Lesbos. . . . I will give him these, and with them shall go the one I took from him, the daughter of Briseus. And to all this I will swear a great oath that I never entered into her bed and never lay with her as is natural for human people . . .'" — Agamemnon, *Iliad* 9:115

You never discuss your business with them, never talk about the thing that occupies most of your thoughts and time, not just because they won't understand, not just because they will find it boring, not just because, in their naïveté, they will criticize you for your practices, for winning, for generating the wealth they are enjoying at that very moment, but because it will pollute them, make them dirty, just as it did with that first one, that one you kept around the longest, that one you mistook for love.

The porn movie industry grosses more annually worldwide than the legitimate movie industry.

And still porn stars say they "make their real money" on tour — all cash.

Also all cash are the strip clubs and most hookers.

All told, in the United States, the sex industry grosses more than the domestic revenue of the tobacco and alcohol industries put together. All told, the American male spends more money annually per capita on the sex industry than on taking his wife to the movies and buying video games for his children. All told, the American male is clearly not getting what he wants at home.

She gives you a ring or a bracelet that says "Peace," or, "Dream more." And you wear it. You wear it even though your friends see it and say, "What the hell is that?" and, embarrassed, because you know exactly how ridiculous it is, you say, "She gave it to me," and then they say, "Oh," and leave it at that because now it makes sense. Yes, you wear it all the time. But you know it will not work. That is what she is for.

"'Agamemnon offers you worthy recompense if you change from your anger.'" — Odysseus to Achilles, *Iliad* 9:260

A mother catches you looking at her daughter. She scowls, she knows what you are thinking because she knows what her husband is thinking when he looks at his daughter's friends. Yet she scowls more when she sees her daughter returning the gaze.

Apollo and Daphne. Merlin and Nimue. Othello and Desdemona. JFK and Marilyn. At what point did enchantment become sin?

I don't remember when exactly but it must have been soon after we'd met, you taught me that if you fold a dollar bill lengthwise and then flatten it out again, a vending machine will almost always accept it.

Goddamn you for that. There are so many people I have forgotten, people I liked much more than you, people that I never even knew I knew until someone else mentions them and I wonder what happened to them because I liked them. But not you. You I must now remember in every airport, in every gymnasium, in every stairwell. Thanks to your little trick, I can never forget you. Goddamn you for that.

Love, lust, passion, longing, a sight for sore eyes, tempted by, weakness for, ache for, pant for, hurt for, languish for, cry for, itch for, wild for, yearning, craving, thirsting, coveting, hungry for, voracious, rapacious, unquenchable, insatiable, stuck on, gone on, need, want, set on, driven mad by, intoxicated, in your blood, besotted, befuddled, drunk, buzzed, bombed, high, stoned, hopped-up, coked-out, fucked, hooked, habit.

Somewhere, sometime, somehow you lose something or see something lost.

If you are lucky it was when you were young. If you are lucky you saw your parents divorced. If you are lucky your high school girlfriend died in a car crash. If you are lucky you saw your little sister lose the use of her legs because your family couldn't afford the right health care.

If you are unlucky, it will happen when you are older. If you are unlucky you will see your son lose his place at the college of his choice to the child of a man richer than you, rich enough to donate some new lab equipment. If you are unlucky your wife of thirty-seven years will develop bipolar disorder and have to be hospitalized after you come home from work and find she has opened her wrists with an electric meat carver. If you are unlucky you will lose your job after twenty-two years of service and will be too old to find another.

If you are unlucky you will realize too late that the way you thought the world worked was just an illusion. If you are unlucky you will become afraid too late.

But if you are lucky you will become afraid when you are young, afraid of the unexpected changing your life for the worse and not having enough power to set things back the way you wanted them to be.

And then, if you are lucky, you will pursue power from that day forth. You will lead armies into Gaul, you will take on a colony in a new world, you will acquire money, you will only maintain relationships where you have the upper hand, only stay in jobs that can eventually lead to you being the one in charge. And you will do this because if you are lucky you will know that power means you don't have to be afraid. Power means you can do what you want when you want to. Power means you can have what you want when you want it.

If you are lucky, you will do this because you will know it is really Power that is worth any sacrifice, that it is really Power without which you can't live, that it is really Power without which you can only eat and breathe and sleep and shit and sometimes not even that. You will do this because if you are lucky you will know that when we say we'd die for Liberty we're really saying we'd die for Power.

Except that in the pursuit of Power one of the things you will have to sacrifice will be the ability to enjoy the thing you lost or saw lost.

So even if you reach that point where you aren't afraid anymore, that point where you can relax, that point where you are free, that point you never reach, even if you reach that point, you will realize you weren't so lucky after all.

Yet, you wonder, who can say they've never been lucky?

Have you ever seen a domesticated dog with his first bone? He will still try to bury it in his bed or the couch or under a skirting board even after all the pushing has worn the top of his nose raw.

You are sitting outside your house in your imported British sports car. It is winter. The sky has just darkened and you have watched the lights come on inside. The trees and the bushes and the statues all around the house remind you of pictures you have seen of spacecraft during re-entry. Every surface, every edge, facing the house glows with yellow light. But beyond that, the objects disappear into darkness, become indistinct.

You had driven up to Boston for a meeting. Normally you would have taken the company jet out of JFK but the car just arrived last weekend. It was the first one on American soil and you got it. So you decided to drive up. You were feeling confident, wanted everyone to see the new car. You were going to let them sit in it if they wanted to. And you knew they'd want to. Besides, Boston was only an hour farther from you than the airport, once you added in the flight time and the trip from Logan to the office, driving almost made things quicker. Almost. And it also might snow soon, then you'd have to wait until spring to take it out again. You refer to the car as "it." You know some men, mostly older men, refer to cars as "her" and "she." You think that's foolish, that it's silly to animate the inanimate.

But then at the meeting, the meeting that was supposed to go well, out of nowhere people started using terms like "scramble" and "rapid repositioning." At one point a COO who had originally been trained in the navy, said, "We got a real SNAFU here." You asked him what the hell that meant anyway and he'd replied, "Situation Normal All Fucked Up."

You had been twenty-five minutes outside of Boston before

you realized you'd forgotten to show everyone the car. They didn't even know you'd driven up.

And now you are looking at the front door, imagining what your wife will want to talk about when you go in. It's not that she's not understanding, she is. As understanding as she could be at least. You know some guys whose wives are a real pain in the ass, whose wives start piling shit on them the moment they walk in the door, whose wives the moment they walk in the door say something like, "You have to talk to that edging man, he won't listen to me." And then, when your friends say, "Can this wait until we've eaten?" when they say, "Can't this wait until I've had a drink? I had a difficult day," their wives say, "Well excuse me! You don't think what I do is hard work? You don't think raising your children and looking after your goddamn house is difficult!?" You know some guys who are so used to this, they don't even bother to answer, they don't even bother to say, "I'm not saying what you do isn't hard work. I'm not saying what you do isn't difficult. I'm not even saying I could do what you do. I'm just saying there wouldn't even be a goddamn house or goddamn children or a goddamn edging man without my work!" You know some guys who don't say any of that. They don't say anything. They just sigh and walk into the closest room with liquor and pour themselves a glass of twenty-five-year-old Highland malt. You even know some guys who would sometimes rather spend a night alone in a hotel in the city, who would sometimes rather go into work the next day in the same clothes than go home.

But your wife isn't like that. She's not like that at all. Your wife is wonderful. She will say "poor dear" if you bother to tell her about today. You frequently don't even have to tell her, frequently she knows how you feel just by looking at your face. She will give you sympathy, stroke your hair, rub soft little circles on that spot on the inside of your elbow. If there are problems with the kids or with the households, she will know enough to keep them to herself until the right time, will even try again to deal with them herself.

And yet tonight when you go to bed, when you lie there awake all night long, your heart pounding like it's going to leap out of your chest as you work and rework your strategy, when you lie there once more trying to figure out how to come out furthest ahead, when you lie there like that, by yourself, she will be sound asleep. And the kids will be sound asleep if they still live at home. And you are happy to give that to them. You really are.

But at some point, perhaps around three or four A.M. after you've gotten up to make yourself a sandwich but have been unable to because you don't know where anything is in your own kitchen, as you return to bed, as you get back in bed and pull the covers up over yourself, you will look down at her and you will wonder what she didn't tell you. You will wonder what other problems you will have to deal with sometime soon, which parts of the things that were supposed to make you happy, which parts of the things that were supposed to fulfill you have gone wrong now. You will wonder what else you will have to deal with on top of the problem that hasn't let you sleep.

And it will occur to you, as you look down at your wonderful, caring, understanding wife, that if she is ever going to really talk at all, if at any point she is ever going to tell you about her life as she once did so long ago (but how long really — ten, fifteen years?), if she's ever going to talk to you as she once talked to you about her classes or her love of sailing or her desire to join the Peace Corps, if she is ever going to talk to you like that again, she will have to talk to you about those responsibilities that she didn't want to talk to you about when you came home tonight. Because they have become her life. Her whole life is now the responsibilities you have made for yourself outside your job. Her whole life is now the world that used to be your dream, the world you have been doing the work to create, the world that has become a burden, the world you now can't bear to face.

And so perhaps looking down at her, something that not so long ago used to fill your face with amazement, sheer disbelief that you were lying naked next to a woman like this, perhaps looking down at her you will suddenly feel sick. Perhaps looking down at her you will suddenly understand why sometimes when you come home and she opens the door with a smile on her face you can't stand the sight of her, why sometimes when that door opens it feels like you've stepped off one unpleasant ride at an amusement park and right onto another one. And perhaps, just perhaps, just for a split second, you will think about how easy it would be to strangle her in her sleep. And then you will wonder where that thought came from.

For no reason at all you run your fingers over the hand-carved wooden dash. You find yourself wondering why British sports cars are so small. Italian and German sports cars are a decent size, why do the British make everything so small, you wonder.

You look at the house again. Then you start the car and go round the circle and out the driveway, hoping no one heard the crunching of the gravel as you went past the front door. You will go for a drink, just one quick drink before you go home.

As you drive, you find yourself wondering if that is why some men never want to marry. Because they are smart enough to know that no matter how well you get along, no matter how well you understand each other, once you start sharing lives completely, wholeheartedly, you must arrive at this point eventually. You wonder if they never want to marry because they are smart enough to know you can only forget about your life in the company of people who are not part of your life.

And as you drive you wonder if it would make a difference if she worked too, if she had a job as stressful as yours, if she too couldn't sleep at night. If perhaps then there'd be some sense of camaraderie, some sense of the two of you battling together against the world. You wonder if things would be better somehow if she worked too. But you doubt it. If she worked too it seems like then, in addition to reminding you of all the responsibilities you have somehow accumulated outside your work, she would also remind you of all the responsibilities you have fought for inside your work. And it also seems like then, if she worked too, when she came home she'd want to talk to you as little as you wanted to talk to her.

You drive past a fast-food restaurant, some place that serves tacos or burgers, some place with a "drive-thru." You realize you haven't eaten all day. You pull in behind a beat-up pickup. A five- or ten-year-old compact pulls in behind you. When you roll down the window to order, the sound of your engine completely drowns the sounds of theirs.

And when you pull up to the drive-thru window, the attendant looks surprised but he doesn't say anything until he hands you your change. Then he can no longer help himself and he says, "Man, if I had a car like that I wouldn't be eating here!" And you smile, and nod, and take your change.

You drive over to a deserted edge of the parking lot and look down at the food he gave you in its paper bag. It's messy and for a second you consider eating it sitting outside on the curb but then you'd definitely ruin the seat of your pants and you don't want to eat inside because you don't want to leave the car alone in this particular parking lot so you tell yourself you'll just be extra careful of the leather and begin eating in the car. But half-way through eating some kind of vegetable squirms loose, some kind of vegetable covered with some kind of sauce, and instinctively you snap your legs together to catch it and it lands in the crotch of your $1,000 pants. And, cursing, you pick it up between thumb and forefinger and open the door with your pinky and your elbow and get out of the car and put the food down on the ground and wipe yourself off with a napkin. It looks OK there and then but in the morning, in the sunlight, you will look at the pants and see that they are ruined. So now you stand there and eat, leaning slightly forward with each bite, and wonder why you didn't think of eating this way before.

And maybe as you eat you look over at a bar across the street, a bar you never really noticed before. It's a little run-down but there are lots of cars around it, the kind of cars that were a good value when they were bought a few years ago, that would be a person's first car or a family's second, the kind of cars that, once they are a few years old, parents give their children when they go away to college. And maybe as you finish your food a new one pulls up and parks outside the bar. And maybe, just maybe, four or five young girls get out, there because this bar doesn't card, there because they know as well as the local police know this bar makes most of its money off underage drinkers. You find yourself wondering how you can tell they're young from this distance when you can't even see the make of their car. They are overdressed for the kind of bar they are going to, wear cocktail dresses, have spent time on their hair. Even from across the street you can tell they spent time on their hair. Even from across the street you can tell they are looking to get laid.

And maybe when you are done eating, you find yourself driving across the street to the bar. It's as good as anywhere, right? You're just going to have one drink and head home probably anyway. Why bother driving another five miles to the only bar within forty miles that serves the scotch you like? And if there's a little something to look at while you drink, so much the better.

You park around back, away from the other cars and out of sight of the street. You figure that's less risky than leaving the car in the parking lot where it might get hit or where someone could see it from the street and might try to steal it. Who's going to know it's even there around back?

And maybe when you go inside, leaving your jacket and tie in the car, maybe the girls you think you saw getting out of the car are playing pool. And maybe for some reason, after you finish your first drink, after everyone in the bar has long since stopped staring at you, you find yourself putting your name on the board. And maybe you end up playing pool with those girls.

After the break, after they overcome their initial shyness, after they are done speculating in whispers among themselves about what you're doing in their bar, the boldest one of them, skeptical for some reason, asks you what you do. "So what do you do anyway?" she asks.

And when you tell them, trying to put it as simply as possible, they all look a little confused except one girl who ventures, "Is that like a kind of merchant banking?"

And when you tell her that merchant banking is very similar to what you do she nods and says, "Yeah, I saw a movie about that once."

And then they all start talking to you, asking you about what you do, where you went to college, where you live, whether you've been to certain places and what they're like if you have. And for some reason you discover you are proud when you give the answers to these questions, answers that only an hour ago depressed you to even think about let alone say out loud. One of them knows your house, says, "Not that huge place you can only just see from the road?" They all start talking to you except the bold girl who first spoke to you. She sits and talks to three or four boys who sit nearby, boys she and her friends obviously already know a little bit. For a little while, the boys don't even look at you, or if they do it's just a disgusted glance. But then, when you start buying rounds of expensive drinks, drinks they could never afford, when you include them in those rounds, when you start actually enjoying your money for the first time in as long as you can remember, they suddenly want to talk to you, are suddenly standing near you instead of on the other side of the table like the girls, lean over your shoulder and give you advice on your shots, ask you questions about your business as if they already knew all about it, questions that always end in "right?" or begin with "But don't you think . . ."

At one point two of the boys head for the bathroom, arguing about what you meant by something, but, finding it full and unable to wait, they go outside to pee.

And they come back in saying, "Dude! Is that your car out there?! It's awesome!" And the girls see that the boys they were so impressed by a few hours ago are impressed by you, by the fact that a certain thing belongs to you. They ask them about it, what is so special about it. And the boys talk about it, know its specifications far better than you do. Except the gas mileage, the one specification you do know, the one specification you have calculated. For the gas mileage they only know the fictional figure written in the handbook. One of them mentions the price among the list of numbers he reels off. Of course, he forgets to include the tax, and the import fees, and the fact that these cars are so hard to get that the dealer asked 15 percent over sticker on yours, he forgets these numbers the sum of which would be enough to pay for a year of his college tuition and living expenses. The other, in response to a question from one of the girls, says, "Let's just say that that's more power than you could ever possibly need."

Then one of the boys, one who didn't go outside, asks if they can sit in it. And you are surprised, strangely thrilled. "Sure!" you say. "If you want to."

And everyone troops outside to see the car. The girls stand back a little while the boys crowd around. As they take their turns sitting in the driver's seat, you notice the mud on their shoes but don't say anything – you don't want to seem too uptight, uncool. Then you remember the box of cigars you had taken up to Boston, illegal cigars, cigars that each cost more than these kids would probably spend in three days on food. And you get it out and unseal it and offer them around. The boys each take one, the girls share one.

Back inside, the boys look at you after their first drags, after they hold their first drags in their mouths too long, and nod and say, "Wow," and "Great," as if they knew. And they stubbornly finish them even though one of them looks a little green by the time he is done. The girls don't even finish the one between them, it ends up smoldering, an abandoned wet little stump with rings of clashing lipstick.

And maybe, just maybe, you catch one of the girls looking at you, the one who saw the movie once, catch her not joining in the conversation around her, looking at you with a serious expression. She looks away in a hurry. And later you see her friends teasing her quietly. And maybe, just maybe, as it gets late, she asks if you'll take her back to campus. You agree — after all, why not, you're not too drunk to drive. You wouldn't do it if you were, you're not irresponsible, you don't want to go to jail.

And as you drive, she talks to you. She is done with questions about you, she knows everything about you she needs to know, wants to know, would even understand. Instead she begins to talk about herself incessantly. And for some reason you are fascinated, not bored as you are when women your own age talk like this. You could listen to her talk about her problems endlessly, about her grades, about her parents, about her teachers, not just because her problems aren't really problems, not just because you know everything will be fine, but, you realize, because her problems have nothing to do with you, because her life has nothing to do with your life. And when she talks about her hopes, about how she wants to be a veterinarian, you can listen and smile and nod and say "that would be exciting" or "I've been there, it's beautiful in the spring" because they are still hopes, because they have not yet become worries. Because her hopes remind you hope exists at all.

And maybe, just maybe, she asks if you want to see her room. And that's the moment when you realize you need to make a decision. That's the moment when you ask yourself what you are doing here, what you are going to do here. That's the moment when you realize you haven't been thinking about the "SNAFU" since you started playing pool, when you realize you haven't thought about the front door to your house opening since you started talking to this girl and her friends.

But when you actually find yourself in her room, her room with a poster of some obscure independent film and a stuffed koala on her bed, her room with a picture of only her mother and her siblings on her desk, her room with the former family computer, you have second thoughts, feel awkward, out of place, like you shouldn't be there, like you should be ashamed to be there. You begin thinking that maybe you've made a mistake, that this is undignified. But then in one smooth, practiced motion, she slips her dress off over her head, reveals those breasts that look like they are actually trying to leap free from their confinement, walks over to you in her underwear and stands on tiptoe and sticks her tongue in your mouth while she starts to undo your belt and you forget all about that.

And maybe, just maybe, underneath her panties, she has a tattoo of a red teddy bear walking in profile on its hind legs. And maybe, just maybe, seeing how crazy it makes you, she jerks you off on it. And then maybe she scoops up some of your semen and, looking right at you, licks it off the ends of her fingers. It has been years since your wife — your wonderful, understanding wife — has done anything like that.

"'For as I detest the doorways of Death, I detest that man, who hides one thing in the depths of his heart, and speaks forth another.'" — Achilles, *Iliad* 9:312

And even the nicest girls we sleep with, the ones we find the most charming, the ones our families ask us about, say, "What happened to Jenni — she was so nice." Even they love it when we abuse them in bed. Yes, abuse them. Even they ask questions like, "Am I your slut? Your whore? Your dirty bitch?" and then shudder when you say, "Yes . . . yes." Even they ask us to tie them up, to blindfold them, to use them.

And if they don't like it, if you use those words and they stop moving, put their hand on your mouth, say, "Don't say that — don't use that word — I don't like it," if they say they don't want to try being handcuffed to the towel rack in the bathroom, they're never any good in bed. They may be brilliant. They may be nice. They may be witty, charming, etc., etc. They may be doing something for women's liberation (over what? over whom?). But they're never any good in bed.

And it's not because we feel threatened, it's not because they're taking control. It's not because of that and that's not what they're doing anyway. Every man likes a dominant woman once in a while, a woman to order him around, to tell him what to do in bed, to say, "Eat my pussy," and, "Good. Now fuck me. But don't cum until I tell you to." Some men like that all the time.

No, it's because they want there to be a balance of power. They want things to be equal. It's because they don't understand good sex has nothing to do with equality.

It may seem like a minor thing when we tip a waitress a little more because she smiles.

It may seem like a minor thing that corporations employ more beautiful women in sales than in other departments.

It may seem like a minor thing that being a centerfold has become a perfectly legitimate route to celebrity.

These all may seem like minor things.

And when we began looking for a house, you loved everywhere. You loved the place where the kitchen was too small. You loved the place with no land. You loved the place next to the school yard.

Eventually I teased you about it and you said, "It's because anywhere will be wonderful if we live there together so it doesn't matter what it's like." I let you choose in the end, I also didn't think it mattered what it was like.

Before we moved the furniture in, you insisted we have sex in every room. "To baptize it," you said. "To make it special."

"'A man dies still if he has done nothing, as one who has done much. Nothing is won for me, now that my heart has gone through its afflictions in forever setting my life on the hazard of battle. For as to her unwinged young ones the mother bird brings back morsels, wherever she can find them, but as for herself it is suffering, such was I, as I lay through all the many nights unsleeping, such as I wore through the bloody days of the fighting, striving with warriors for the sake of these men's women. . . .

'All the other prizes of honour he gave the great men and the princes are held fast by them, but from me alone, of all the Achaians he has taken and keeps the bride of my heart. Let him lie beside her and be happy. Yet why must the Argives fight with the Trojans? And why was it the son of Atreus assembled and led here these people? Was it not for the sake of lovely-haired Helen? Are the sons of Atreus alone among mortal men the ones who love their wives? Since any who is a good man, and careful, loves her who is his own . . . as I . . . though it was my spear that won her.'" — Achilles, *Iliad* 9:320

You look in the mirror — you take care of yourself but you still have those ridges now, they have grown above your pelvis.

They are not ugly, exactly, but they are weight. You cannot make them go away.

One out of every two marriages ends in divorce.

Four out of five spouses admit to cheating on their partner — we don't know how many of the remaining 20 percent are simply not admitting it.

Thousands of people are employed by sports teams and film shoots and companies, by men with enough money, to "look after" wives. Ostensibly their job is to make sure the wives are happy and comfortable and get taken shopping, whether it's to exclusive local hand-painted scarf boutiques or to remote villages known for their blue-glazed pottery. But in reality their job is to assist in keeping the wives away from the husbands when the husbands want to "play." And, truth be told, the majority of the wives know precisely what these "assistants" are being paid for, the majority of the wives have no illusions.

So who is it, exactly, that we think we're fooling?

She lets you — no, wants you to take dirty pictures of her. "Come on!" she says. "Just for you," she says, "you know, for when we can't be together."

So there you are. Hiding from your wife. On a Wednesday night in one of your eleven bathrooms with your Armani pants around your ankles. A forty-two-year-old man worth hundreds of millions of dollars, a king, masturbating like a schoolboy over a single page torn from *Hustler* because you can't wait for the weekend.

Except it isn't a page from a magazine. It's a Polaroid of her on the beach. You have others but this is your favorite. She is leaning back against a large rock. It is craggy and ferrous, an enormous glossy clot. Just to the left of it, at the edge of the picture, in the distance on the white beach, people can be made out sunbathing, families. The beach is so white they seem like drawings on a piece of paper. You don't remember framing the picture so they could be seen, you're almost certain you didn't mean to. She is wearing the bikini you bought her, the $340 bikini that is mostly little ropes. With her right hand she is lifting her left breast up and out of the bikini, towards her tiny mouth, her extended, curled tongue. Her head is bent down as far as it will go, her blond hair cascading, veiling the right side of her body down to her stomach. Her eyes are closed. Her left hand is thrust inside her bikini bottoms. Her hair and her tongue glisten as do the most polished, most metallic edges of the rock forming a drunken spider's web behind her. If you look closely, and you have, you can see the sun reflected in her tongue stud. A brilliant, painful point.

There are so many things about this picture that can make you cum. The fact that her eyes are closed as if she were in a deep and dreamless sleep. The metal in her tongue so close to the puckered, pink flesh of her nipple. Her tan right arm curving across her body, striped like a tiger by her hair. And, perhaps most of all, her bikini bottoms raised into ridges by her fingers, the highest peak the bump of what you know is the middle joint of her middle finger, poised to push into herself.

She's mad to take risks like that, crazy. Masturbating behind a rock on a crowded beach and letting you take pictures of her. Doesn't she understand she — you — we — could get caught? Doesn't she understand exactly how close to the edge we all are? But then, she has nothing to lose. And it is because she is mad that you must be with her. Because her madness is infectious.

When you are done you are suddenly filled not with guilt but with terror. You are afraid someone might somehow find the pictures. Afraid you will go to jail. Afraid you will lose everything you have. But most of all, you are afraid of the embarrassment. No one will understand everything she is to you, that she is everything to you, that she is worth the risk, that without her everything you have is nothing. No one will understand any of this. You will just be someone who made an underage girl pose for dirty pictures, someone who collected child pornography.

And you swear to yourself you'll get rid of the pictures first thing in the morning. You swear to yourself that this time it's just for the night you're putting them back in their strongbox which is itself in the safe in your study.

And you may even keep your promise. It's possible that your resolve will in fact remain in the morning. That you'll burn them.

But a few weeks later, she'll convince you to take some more in the back stacks at a public library. And she won't have to try very hard.

"'I have many possessions there that I left behind when I came here on this desperate venture, and from here there is more gold, and red bronze, and fair-girdled women, and grey iron I will take back; all that was allotted to me. But my prize; he who gave it, powerful Agamemnon, son of Atreus, has taken it back again outrageously. Go back and proclaim to him all that I tell you, openly . . . wrapped as he is forever in shamelessness; yet he would not, bold as a dog though he be, dare look in my face any longer.

'I will join with him in no counsel, and in no action. He cheated me and he did me hurt. Let him not beguile me with words again . . . not if he gave me gifts as many as the sand or the dust is, not even so would Agamemnon have his way with my spirit until he made good to me all this heartrending insolence.

'Nor will I marry a daughter of Atreus' son, Agamemnon . . . not if she matched the work of her hands with grey-eyed Athena . . . . For if the gods will keep me alive, and I win homeward, Peleus himself will presently arrange a wife for me. There are many Achaian girls in the land of Hellas and Phthia, daughters of great men who hold strong places in guard. . . . And the great desire in my heart drives me rather in that place to take a wedded wife in marriage, the bride of my fancy, to enjoy with her the possessions won by aged Peleus.

'For not worth the value of my life are all the possessions they fable were won for Ilion, that strong-founded citadel, in the old days when there was peace. . . . Of possessions cattle and fat sheep are things to be had for the lifting, and tripods can be won, and the tawny high heads of horses, but a man's life cannot come back again, it cannot be lifted nor captured again by force, once it has crossed the teeth's barrier.

'For my mother Thetis the goddess of the silver feet tells me I carry two sorts of destiny toward the day of my death. Either, if I stay here and fight beside the city of the Trojans, my return home is gone, but my glory shall be everlasting; but if I return home to the beloved land of my fathers, the excellence of my glory is gone, but there will be a long life left for me, and my end in death will not come to me quickly.'" — Achilles, *Iliad* 9:364

You are visiting St. Peter's with your wife. You haven't been married very long. You bought a new camera for this little vacation. It is impossibly small, a spy camera, very expensive. In the basilica, your wife overhears a couple about your own age speaking English and asks them if they'd take a picture of you. When she hands the woman the camera, she is fascinated by it. She can't believe how small it is. "Look how small it is!" she says to her husband. They are dressed differently from the two of you, in clothes sold in large stores where entire families can shop. He just nods and says, "Uh-huh." Then your wife, thrilled with the camera to begin with, eager to show it off to someone else who appreciates it, says, "Isn't it great? And look — it does this and this and this." And she shows the other woman all the things this camera does, this camera that is so well machined it resembles the eye of some kind of surgical robot. At last the other woman says to her husband, "Honey — we have to get one of these!"

And before he replies he looks at you and shakes his head slightly and rolls his eyes, then he says without looking at his wife, flashing his eyes and his eyebrows briefly up to heaven, "Oh sure, honey, no problem, we'll pick one up this afternoon. . . ." And she laughs but you know he'll hear about that camera for some time. And always when he least expects it. And you know he'll never be able to buy her one. And you suddenly feel very bad for him. You suddenly want to take him aside and slip him the money for the camera — nothing to you, almost spare change — and say, "Here, here you go, get her the camera." But you know you could never do that. You know that would be even more embarrassing. You know that would damage his pride. You know that would change his camaraderie to resentment, that that would destroy the moment the two of you shared when, without speaking he said, "I don't hate you for being able to give your wife something my wife wants because I know your wife wants things you can't give her. I know that no matter how much we have, it is never enough. I know that if she had the camera, she'd want your tennis court." So you just feel bad for him and leave it at that.

And then, once the picture's taken, as you part ways and wander off towards the dome, your wife says, "They seemed like a nice couple, didn't they?"

All over the world, we see dead people. Everywhere we go, we visit graves and cemeteries and cities of the dead, we take excursions to tombs or pyramids or burial mounds or stupas, we make a point of seeing at least one monument, one cenotaph, one cromlech, one battlefield before we take our leave. Even on vacation we not only can't get away from death, we seek it out. Even on vacation, there are epitaphs everywhere we look.

In New Orleans, you sit outside at the Café du Monde. White paint peels from the pillars around you as it would in any formerly Spanish territory. Their shadows are long across the small metal tables, long, but growing shorter. You drink chicory coffee, eat beignets that send clouds of powdered sugar into the air. You are always surprised at how many of them you can eat without feeling ill. You must always actually tell yourself to stop or you never would.

When you see her you don't recognize her at first. Instead, you suddenly smell rose jelly, black tea. You look around but of course the Café du Monde serves neither. You smile to yourself and wonder why you think you smell those things here, now, things you have not tasted since you were in Istanbul, since the last time you saw Elena. And it is in remembering her that you recognize her. It is her across the street by the light. It is her waiting to cross Decatur.

Yes, she is wearing the same kind of oversize aviators she made famous so long ago. Yes, she is even wearing a vintage miniskirt and halter top of the kind you shot her in so many times. But she is still hard to recognize.

You watch her cross the street, watch her walk onto the Café terrace, but you do not say anything. You think she has seen you but does not recognize you. She sits near you, perhaps even at the table next to yours. Still you say nothing. What is there to say? When her coffee and beignets arrive, she takes off her sunglasses. Anyone who bothered to look would see she has been crying.

As you watch her sip her coffee, more of Istanbul comes back to you — a coffeehouse across from the Hagia Sofia dense with the violet smoke of apple tobacco and the clac-clac-clac of backgammon, the men staring at you, at her, the only woman, the shout of the muezzin coming from the mosque — more of Istanbul and the other times you saw her during those two years you were both in Europe. The time in Paris with the balcony doors open when, through the iron railing, across the street, you could make out a woman doing her ironing as you fucked her. The time in the Aegean on the deck of Sergei's yacht when, after everyone else had gone to bed, you had to cover her mouth with the palm of your hand before she drowned out the slap of the waves against the hull. And, of course, the first time, the time you tried again just to be sure.

You were outside Barcelona. On a beach of black sand and flashing mica, a beach that looked nothing like the night sky, you took pictures of her. It was the last day of the shoot but she wore sunglasses as she had every other day. That was her thing, why people called her. That was the summer those glasses became popular. Everyone had to have them in their shoot; no one made them look as plausible as her. Hidden, her face launched dozens of summer lines. And after that last day was over, a half day, the two of you walked through the medieval part of the city. That was when you tried again. Even though she'd rebuffed your first couple of attempts, you tried again just to be sure. After all, this wasn't just another model. This was a girl Daimon Lake had chosen to be seen with more than once. Even if she hadn't been a model, even if she'd been ugly, you still might have tried. Those things mattered to you then. So on the steps of the old cathedral you said, "Just a minute," and, "May I?" and you reached out with both hands and took off her sunglasses. Then you took a picture of her on the steps, in the setting sun, took a picture of her and said as you lowered the camera, "It's a shame. It really is. A shame." After dinner, in an armchair near your bed, she fucked you for the first time.

She puckers her face at her first sip. The coffee too bitter, she pours sugar, asks for milk. You remember her first phone call to you in Sapporo. The line kept breaking up, they weren't as good then as now. For her it was morning, for you, night. She was calling from New York. She told you how when she'd gotten back there'd been messages for her from Daimon. How he'd asked her to go to the Oscars with him, to be his date at the Oscars. "The Oscars, Alex," she'd said. "I hope you don't mind," she'd said. "I won't sleep with him or anything." But you knew she hadn't told him about you.

"Be careful," you said.

"I will," she replied. But she thought you were talking about drugs, about red sports cars, about rape.

Then she said, "Hello? . . . Hello? . . . Something funny just happened to the line — I can't hear you anymore . . . are you there? Alex — if you can hear me I'll call you from L.A., OK? I'll call you from L.A.," she'd shouted and hung up.

She takes a careful bite of a beignet but she did call you from Los Angeles. She called you to tell you about the dresses. Dozens of designers had been sending her couture. She could keep it if she wore it to the awards or even to any of the parties just before or after. She called you just to tell you she'd spent the last three days trying on one-offs in her hotel room, a room Daimon had paid for.

"Don't worry about it — it's just another slut run — that's all," she said. That was what her and her friends had called it when, back in high school, they'd get dressed up and ask an older man to buy them beer and cigarettes. She'd told you that the previous October, in Berlin, strolling near the Wall. Shortly before you had both agreed you felt sorry for those on the other side.

"Live by the sword . . . ," you'd replied. You still said things like that then, still bothered trying to be clever. In the snow, near an assassinated shogun's mausoleum, you had been photographing winter coats. She'd laughed, told you you could be so weird sometimes.

When you came in last night, you'd noticed the HMIs lighting up the Ursuline convent. The shoot must be Daimon's, she must be traveling with him for once. She rubs her fingers quickly back and forth against her thumb. The powdered sugar. She called you a few more times. She called you to ask you if you could believe it about the paparazzi outside the restaurants, if you could believe they couldn't get enough of her and Daimon. She called you to tell you you would never believe that someone had asked her to autograph a spread in *Vogue*. And, of course, she called you the day after to tell you about the television cameras and the interviews they said were broadcast worldwide, to tell you about the giant Oscar statues flanking the entrance to the auditorium and who she met at all the parties.

But that was all. She never called you after that. She never called you to tell you she had moved in to Daimon's mansion in Malibu. She never called you to tell you he had asked her to marry him. She never called you to tell you that, the night he proposed, as she fell asleep, the taste of Cointreau and semen still in her mouth, she thought, "This must be the way they all felt, all those Queens and Princesses, this must be exactly the way they all felt." She never called you to tell you any of that. She never called you again.

Not that it mattered to you, not that you cared. By then you'd been wise enough to also move on. By then you were in England. By then you were photographing the steps of St. Paul's, of Westminster, of Canterbury.

She reaches into her purse, withdraws some eyedrops. She

throws her head back. The wattle on her neck tightens a little but not all the way down to her sternum. Her blouse is very low cut. You've heard a couple things about her since then. It would have been impossible for you not to, you move in such similar circles.

An executive chef you know once said he'd seen her on the beach in Rio throwing a sandal. She was wearing a sarong and yelling, "You bastard, you fucking bastard!" She had taken the shoe off to throw it at Daimon. He backed away from her, palms held up and out in front of him. He laughed as if he'd played a practical joke on her, nothing more. She'd missed, had hit another woman sunbathing.

A producer friend of yours lives in their building on Fifth Avenue. One time he told you he came home to find something of a riot on the street side. When he asked someone what was going on they just said, "It's raining diamonds, man, diamonds!" and returned to scouring the gutter. He found out from the doorman that Elena had thrown all her jewelry out the window. The tenants across the hall had heard her yelling at Daimon, asking him how he could expect it to mean anything to her.

And, of course, your old assistant now does their daughter's publicity shots. She (the daughter) can't keep her mouth shut. She tells him how her mother won't file for divorce because of the pre-nup, how she'd be left with nothing. No money, no contacts, no skills, no friends. She tells him how her father is paying paternity to at least three other women. She tells him how her mother is more of an employee than anything else, that she looks after her and the houses and the staff and receives a monthly allowance.

The eyedrops run down her cheeks. Her eyes remain bloodshot. And you find yourself wondering if you should have done more. After all, you knew. Perhaps you should have told her in what ways her expectations were flawed, perhaps you should have told her what kind of arrangement she was making. But as she puts the eyedrops back in her purse you decide there was, in reality, nothing more you could have done, nothing more you could have said. Because she wouldn't have listened. After all, Daimon wasn't the one taking advantage of her.

Now she dabs at her cheeks with a handkerchief, checks her foundation in a gold compact. You look at your watch. It is almost time to go.

You finish your coffee, look at the last beignet, tell yourself not to eat it. "Let's go," you say to your companion.

"Awww . . . do we have to? I'm tired," she pouts. You almost give in.

"No," you say, "I mean, 'yes,' yes, we have to — the Presbytère is right over there, it's not far . . . besides, I know this creative director, he'll get all pissy if we don't start when he wanted us to." "Come on," you add, standing up, putting a bill on the table.

She huffs but she obeys, gets up. As she bends over to pick up her bag all the men that can see her stare. Her skirt falls just short of revealing her panties. She has long legs and her hair ripples in the sun when she bends down, stands up. But her real signature is her lips. She has wonderfully full lips. "Blowjob lips" you called them when you told the creative director about her.

Your motion draws Elena's attention. She has put away her compact and is staring at you over the cup of coffee she holds to her mouth. She is studying you, frowning. She examines the girl you're with as if checking a fact, a number in a ledger. Your companion notices, stares back at her, but not in the same way. She seems to be looking at a creature under glass in a museum she didn't want to visit.

Terrified, you quickly turn your back, pat your companion on her firm little ass, say, "Let's go." No one calls out your name as you weave your way through the tables. No one runs to catch up with you out on the sidewalk. You seem to have escaped. But just to be sure, you decide to go round the long way, via Madison. Just to be sure, you avoid walking along the railing, avoid getting any closer to her than is absolutely necessary.

At the curb, as she slips her hand into yours, as she looks first one way then the other, as she looks to see if you might jaywalk instead of waiting for the light, your companion says lightly, "God, did you see the woman next to us? Did you see that blouse?! What on earth was she thinking? She should have a little more respect. . . ."

Once, early on, I called in sick when I wasn't sick.

Once, we rented a car for the day and drove up the Hudson Valley.

Once we looked at antiques and had lunch and went for a walk in the woods.

Once I stuck wildflowers in my nose and made you laugh.

Once, still laughing, you pushed me down on some leaves and collapsed on top of me and suddenly stopped laughing and looked very serious all of a sudden and said, "Promise me you'll tell me if you ever stop loving me."

Once you assumed that, at some point, I had started.

Once I said, "I promise, I promise."

The ancient Greeks had no word for romantic love. To them, love for a thing and love for a woman were one and the same. When speaking or writing of a man's relationship to a woman they used words that meant "owned," "valued highly," or "had sex with." When Odysseus returned home, he and Penelope did not cuddle. They fucked.

Very occasionally they would employ the word "mingle" to refer to intercourse, but even then the most striking example of this is when the bones of Achilles and Patroclus are mingled together in death.

Aphrodite was not the goddess of love as is popularly believed, as we tell our children. She was the Goddess of Sex. The patron goddess of prostitutes in fact. And her son, Eros, dear little Cupid with his darling little arrows, was the god of passion.

And this is why even Sappho spoke only of longing, of pain, of sex, of people being precious to her, this is why even Sappho never used the word "love." It didn't exist.

The Romans were the first to suggest there may be one more kind of love. For the most part, the Latin word *amare* (that verb we all learned to conjugate by repeating over and over: *amo, amas, amat,* etc.) combined the meanings of the two Greek words *eros* and *agape.* It could be used to imply a sexual relationship between two people, self-love, the love of possessions, or the love between friends, relations, and nations. However, it does seem possible to make the argument that very occasionally it could have also implied a relationship between husband and wife that was somehow distinct from both friendship and sexual desire. But it is hard to make a solid case for this. After all, the Romans obviously did not see this kind of relationship as distinct enough to deserve its own word. In addition, if the texts of the most famous Latin "love" stories are read closely, it is clear they are not talking about anything more than intense sexual desire. Dido's relationship with Aeneas, for example, begins with sex in a cave during a thunderstorm and is referred to as both "wild" and "improper." Why "improper"? Because she had been previously married and the Romans, perhaps coincidentally, were also the first to introduce the concept of *univira,* the rule that a woman could only ever have one husband. It may also be nothing more than coincidence that the Romans colloquially employed *amare* to mean "be obliged to."

So the word "love" that we use today we did not get from Latin or Greek, but from Anglo-Saxon. It first appeared in the ninth century and, as far as can be understood today, seems to have been used to mean "the care one feels for something precious that one already owns," as distinguished from "lust" (also from Anglo-Saxon) which meant "the desire for something precious that one does not already own." Thus both love and lust could be felt equally for gems, horses, or women, and in equal fashion.

In English, then, "love" first came to refer to a relationship between two people, as opposed to between a person and a thing, because of Christian doctrine. As time progressed, the word was taken up as the translation of the Latin *amare* in its context of "goodwill between men."

Subsequent and consequent to this, during the age of chivalry, once Christian morality had gained a firm foothold and sex outside of wedlock was considered a sin, "love" became employed as the euphemism for sex. A writer could refer to the "love" between an unwedded man and woman (or two men or two women) without fear of reprisal. Not so an explicit reference to sexual intercourse out of wedlock, a situation that would not change for over half a millennium. Hence Malory speaks of Lancelot's "love" for Guinevere despite the fact that the relationship he actually describes seems to amount to little more than the odd fumbling rut in the back stairwells of Camelot.

"Love" can be said to have finally assumed its modern sense in Elizabethan times. And who's to say if this meaning would have endured so long were it not for Shakespeare's popularization of that meaning. Shakespeare, whose work has been translated into as many languages as the Bible. Shakespeare, who was, after all, writing for his queen.

So believe me when I tell you love is the printing press and the arcade version of Centipede. Believe me when I tell you that, at the very best, love is a brand-new thing.

Because no matter how often we cancel the trip, say, "No, you guys go on, I'm just going to relax at the lodge," decide to do something quiet instead, no matter how often we can't find the energy for other things, we always have the energy to fuck them. Whenever we have an opportunity to fuck them, the energy finds us.

The global sex slave trade grosses more annually than the global drug trade.

You've only ever had one experience that far surpassed your expectations even though it was the one experience you always imagined (just like every other straight man you've ever known) would be far better than any other.

It wasn't the first time you tasted Beluga caviar.

It wasn't the first time you dove the Great Barrier Reef.

It wasn't the first time you held the first unique codex in your collection.

It wasn't even the first time you paid two hookers to have sex with you and each other all at the same time.

It was the time back when you had been dating a bisexual girl for quite some time so you felt close to her, knew her quite well, intimately even, and you took her and an old girlfriend of hers out to dinner and just like one of those stories in *Penthouse* the three of you ended up in bed together. Except it wasn't like one of those stories in *Penthouse.* It was better. It was, in fact, the only thing you've ever known for which there was no "like" or even "a little bit like," for which there was no "you know how you feel when." It was the only thing you've ever known for which there were no words at all. It was the only experience you've ever had during which your mind was blank throughout, during which you thought nothing throughout. Nothing. During which, throughout, you simply existed, or, perhaps, ceased to exist.

"' . . . I first left Hellas, the land of fair women, running from the hatred of Ormenos' son Amyntor, my father; who hated me for the sake of a fair-haired mistress. For he made love to her himself, and dishonoured his own wife, my mother; who was forever taking my knees and entreating me to lie with this mistress instead so that she would hate the old man. I was persuaded and did it; and my father when he heard of it straightway called down his curses, and invoked against me the dreaded furies that I might never have any son born of my seed . . . so that it was you, godlike Achilleus, I made my own child, so that some day you might keep hard affliction from me.'" — Phoenix, *Iliad* 9:447

And yet sometimes it is not condescension, sometimes we really do enjoy their company. Sometimes, when they talk about their three-month stay on a Navajo reservation or their volunteer work on emissions control, we find them endearing. Like a child noticing fire hydrants or telephone lines and pointing them out to us.

And also like that child they make us see what we haven't seen in years, what we couldn't remember ever seeing until they pointed it out. And in the seeing is rejuvenation, for what is being a child if not seeing like a child?

And that is why we follow them sometimes, why we let them lead us around, why we let them do that even when our friends start saying, "You?! You're going to a pro-choice rally?! She really has you whipped, doesn't she? Of course, I don't blame you — if I had a piece of tail like that I'd do anything she wanted too." But they're wrong. It's not that you're doing what she wants it's that she makes you want what she does, reminds you that you used to want those things too, reminds you not everyone was always the way you are now not even yourself, makes you feel like there is a point to those pointless battles she has the energy to fight, makes you feel good about yourself again, makes you think once more that maybe your life could have some meaning after all. Like your high school soccer coach once made you believe you could win the last game after you'd lost all season, she makes you believe.

But if your own daughter came to you, your own daughter who is, you've calculated, older than she is by fifteen weeks, if she came to you and said she wanted to spend the summer before her senior year working for the Red Cross outside Calcutta, you'd tell her she was being ridiculous. You'd tell her it was a waste of time, that she had to take the internship you arranged for her at your attorney's firm. You'd tell her the sooner she knew what the real world was like, the sooner she knew what it took to survive, the better. You'd tell her not everyone is lucky enough to have the opportunities she does.

The Lamia is considered by many to be the first example of a vampire in folklore and mythology because she drank the blood of her victims.

The Lamia, however, killed her victims out of spite, not necessity.

The Lamia was not a revenant.

The Lamia commanded no supernatural talents, she could not, for example, change shape at will, she did not possess enormous strength.

The Lamia was not able to pass as a member of society.

In fact, if we look closely, the Lamia is really part of that mythology to which the Harpies, the Scylla, and eventually the New England witch belong, that mythology in which a monster in the form of the opposite sex threatens to destroy us. If we look closely it is, in fact, obvious that the Lamia is not part of that mythology in which a monster draws something from contact with youth (usually sexual contact and preferably virginal youth) that will give it power, or, at the very least, sustain it in a state of undeath. It is difficult, for example, to trace a line between the Lamia and the immensely popular modern Japanese hentai manga or anime in which normal men are transformed into demons by the sight of schoolgirls whose prompt rape gives them the strength to remain materialized.

It was when we stopped going to museums. For years we had gone almost every weekend, almost every weekend there was something, somewhere we wanted to see. Then, one weekend, there wasn't. That was when it was over between us. When we stopped going to museums.

And yet we stayed married for years after that. Years. Why did we do that?

"' . . . and Idas . . . was the strongest of all men upon earth in his time; for he even took up the bow to face the King's onset, Phoibus Apollo, for the sake of the sweet-stepping maiden . . .'" — *Iliad* 9:558

You remember your first report card from high school. Your home room teacher had written under the general comments section, "Less Romeo, more study." Your mother and father told you to listen to what she said, that it was good advice. So you began to study more, you began to do well. And your parents were proud of you and told you so and told all their friends how smart you were, how well you were doing in school.

But that first report card was the only one your father ever actually took out to show his friends.

If you talk to enough porn stars and strippers, or if you read enough interviews with them, you start to realize there is only one thing that is true about them all.

They are not all bimbos. Many are quite witty and more than a few are actually very bright.

They do not all hate their work. Some actually quite enjoy it, think it's fun, can't believe they can get paid for having sex.

They are not all drug addicts. In fact, since HIV, most are strongly against drug use and will refuse to work with anyone who is an addict.

They do not all have low self-esteem. Many are precisely the reverse — very proud, very sure of themselves, so self-reliant for so long, so used to establishing boundaries so often, they don't take shit from anyone, least of all the men they sleep with.

They did not all grow up in broken homes or homes with drug or alcohol problems or homes where they were sexually abused as children. (Although one or more of these things tends to be true in over 95 percent of cases.)

No, the one thing that is true without exception about every porn star or stripper is that they grew up poor.

You are in Amsterdam and you can't believe your virility with this girl. Resigned, long past shame, you had asked them for the youngest girl they had. It is legal to prostitute girls over the age of fifteen in Amsterdam. Some people go there for the legalized drugs. Not you.

One time, a few years ago, you had paid a hooker — a former *Playboy* centerfold — fifteen thousand dollars to go to Key West with you for a weekend. She was, without a doubt, worth every penny. She was spectacularly beautiful, the kind of girl you and your friends thought you would only ever dream of having when you were teenagers. She was highly skilled too, knew how to do everything just right. She had nice clothes, seemed well educated, was not embarrassing at dinner with your friends and their girlfriends and wives. Most of them, the other women, assumed she was your girlfriend. The men, even the men you didn't know at all, knew better. It was your interactions that gave you away. You were too comfortable around her, too relaxed. It was obvious you didn't care what she thought about anything you said or did, obvious you were unafraid of repercussion, unafraid of not getting what you wanted. The two of you were so goddamn friendly with each other. Like two men who have just met but immediately discover they like each other. Yes, she was perfect. And that whole weekend you came maybe, what, four or five times. Certainly by Sunday you were so uninterested you sublet her out to a friend of yours and his wife.

And yet here, in Amsterdam, with this girl, in one night you have cum three times already. This girl they sent up really is young. It's possible she's not even sixteen. The traces of childhood are gone — the gangliness, the spindly limbs and neck, the overlarge eyes — but just barely. Her hips have hardly swollen enough to give her a waist, her breasts will still develop a little more. But God is she sexy. She has the most beautiful eyes, the fullest lips. When you opened your door the thought that she might be too young flashed through your mind for a second, just for a second, but then you dismissed it, asked yourself what that meant anyway, by whose standards, by where's standards, she was capable of carrying a baby wasn't she? In Egypt she would already be a married mother of more than one child. And God is she sexy, you thought. She was squinting slightly as she looked at you, had her face slightly lowered and turned to the left, was looking up at you just a little bit, pouting just a little bit. You couldn't control yourself. You pulled her inside the room, closed the door, and fucked her right there, right up against the door, her clothes still on. And she kissed you. Really kissed you, opened her mouth wide, shoved her tongue in your mouth, couldn't kiss you enough. She wasn't very good at it, messy, unpracticed, your teeth collided, but they were the best kisses you'd ever had. And hookers never kiss you, or if they do, it is controlled, unabandoned, designed to produce a particular effect. It is not for its own sake. This girl, this young hooker, still kissed for its own sake.

And when you were done, you actually felt a little guilty, even you. You looked at her (she looked right back, looked right into your eyes with your cock still inside her, with her arms still around your shoulders, looked right into your eyes and shoved her hips forward and when you nearly collapsed because she did that, when your knees nearly gave out because you were so sensitive, she opened her mouth wide and laughed a hard, happy laugh, smiling and snarling all at once, all with her mouth open wide) you looked at her and thought, "This girl has a problem. This girl is addicted to sex. This girl likes fucking strange men and if she gets paid for it, so much the better." You looked at her and thought, "This girl was probably repeatedly molested when she was a child."

But then she pulled herself off you and walked over to the bed, leaving her skirt hiked up around her waist, not bothering to pull her skirt down, it not even occurring to her that there'd be anything about her body you wouldn't like, that she should be ashamed of anything about her body, showing you that her legs, at least, were fully developed, were very long compared to her torso. But then she undressed and got into your bed. But then she rolled around under the expensive sheets, enjoying their feel against her body. But then she turned over at last and pulled them back to make a space for you and showed you her naked body lying stretched out on its side and beckoned you with one finger and you found you were already getting another erection, found that you were ready to fuck her again. "She must think it's her," you thought as she pulled you into bed by your cock. "She must think men can do it over and over with her because she's sexy or because she's a great fuck. I wonder if she even knows we're not always like this, not always capable of this? If she doesn't, I wonder what she'll think in a few years when her clients start wanting to fuck her only once, maybe twice, and then want her to leave, don't want her to stay the entire night?" You thought all this in a second and then lost yourself in her.

And that time and the last time, after you were done, again the guilt came back, the concern for her. Yes, concern. But then you put your hand on the bone of her hip, saw the curve of her ribs on her side beneath her right breast, saw the back of her knee, and you had to have her again. And every time you reach over to take her again, she laughs that laugh, that cold, hard, satisfied laugh.

Each time the time in between grows longer, to be sure, you worry about her more, but you still manage to fuck her five times that night. You can't believe it. You haven't cum five times in one night since high school.

When she leaves the next morning, sore, walking carefully, her pussy like a wound, you give her double what you agreed on. You do it because she was good, because she earned it, but also because you want to make her life better. Because you do feel sorry for her. But when she takes the money, she is not surprised that you have given her twice what she was supposed to get. She doesn't even think you've made a mistake.

"'. . . but the gods put in your breast a spirit not to be placated, bad, for the sake of one single girl. Yet now we offer you seven, surpassingly lovely, and much beside these. Now make gracious the spirit within you.'" — Telamonian Ajax to Achilles, *Iliad* 9:636

This is why we find those accents so charming — the Southern, the Scottish, the Russian — anything remote, anything that might suggest the ignorance is reinforced, that geography has made it even more extreme than it would have been otherwise.

There is so much sociobiology I could bore you with. For example, I could point out that one would expect women and not men to lose their attractiveness with age since it is only women who lose their ability to breed. Or that the security older men can typically provide their offspring more than compensates for their deteriorated health. Or that most corrections to beauty are not, in fact, abstract aesthetic decisions but rather directed efforts to appear less congenitally hazardous. Or that until the last thirty-odd years (and even then only in developed nations), natural selection would have favored women with the ability to make men care more about protecting and supporting them than other women. You might even find it uninteresting that the more recently they have orgasmed, the better men perform on Mensa entrance exams. Yes, I could tell you about any number of dull things like the altruism gene or R selection or Occam's razor. But I won't. Instead I will just tell you this:

We have known for some time that male mammals are separated from female mammals by a difference in genetic material of about 0.5 percent.

But we have learned only recently that men are separated from mice by a difference in genetic material of no more than about 1 percent.

Which has led us to believe that once we finish mapping the human genome along with those of the higher primates there is a very real chance we will discover men share more genes with male gorillas than they do with women.

We were on the Upper East Side in February about a year before we were divorced. It was a Saturday and we'd been to a classical Greek art gallery on Madison. They had a horse from the Homeric period someone thought I might be interested in. I liked it but pretended I didn't. I was already thinking I might not want you to know about everything I owned, least of all a two-inch iron horse that cost more than a small house and could be easily hidden.

Where we crossed Seventy-second Street, two men were cleaning an asphalt cutter. It was an enormous metal wheel with blunt titanium teeth and mounted on its own vehicle. The men were facing the crosswalk and spraying the cutter down with a hose, their view of the crosswalk blocked. It was cold and the water was freezing where it pooled. As we passed the cutter a bit of spray caught you on your mink. You walked around to the other side of the cutter and said to the men, "Hey, come on, look —" you showed them the wet spot on your coat. "Just be a little careful, OK?" you said. You were trying to be a good sport, trying to let them know that the next person might not be as understanding as you.

I told you to leave them be.

And when we were children, why did we look up four-letter words in the dictionary? Did we think the words could tell us what the things were like?

"Toughen the boy up a little, see if he has what it takes to succeed." You know this is always a good idea but you never think about what it takes or from where. You never think about the fact that, in the end, what it takes is all he will really want.

And yet it takes a puppy some time to become cautious in its approach to other dogs.

A friend calls you. He is younger than you. Not by much but by enough. He is, like you, single. He tells you about this model he's been seeing, an eighteen-year-old he was introduced to by a friend of his. He used to be a model himself in college. He tells you a little bit about her, about how much fun she is, how she wants to "do all these things," and you just keep saying, uh-huh, uh-huh, yeah, because you've heard all this before, you've already been where he's been, because he's telling you about a town you know like the back of your hand. Then he tells you how she just left to go away for a month but when she left she made him "pinky promise" that he'd return her calls when she got back. "Pinky promise!" he repeats. He somehow already knows this is something to boast about. And he's right. It gets even you. "Are you serious?" you say. "'Pinky promise'?! She said that? You lucky motherfucker!" You're jealous because there are so many kinds of eighteen and from just those two little words you know he's stumbled on the best kind of all, the still likes pizza kind, the still collects stuffed animals kind, the pinky promise kind.

"I know, I know," he says, laughing, "but I feel bad, man."

You tell him not to worry about it, that there's nothing to feel bad about. You know he just doesn't quite understand yet.

But he will. And when he does, when he realizes this is something he not only needs but deserves, he'll stop feeling bad.

And as you hang up you can't help thinking how the girl must not understand either, how to have thought it necessary to exact an oath like that, she must think she's lucky someone like your friend, with his money and looks and experience, is even talking to her, how she must think he couldn't possibly be interested in someone her age, someone so inexperienced, someone so young, how she must think he has better things to do, more important things to worry about, how she must wonder what she could possibly give him that he doesn't have already.

You know, as you hang up, she must not have even considered the possibility she has something to give him that he once had but has now lost. And you know this because if she had even an inkling of this possibility, she never would have thought it necessary to use those words in the first place.

And yet, if she didn't think it necessary to use those words, then your friend wouldn't be interested in her. If she didn't think it necessary to use those words, she really would have nothing to offer him.

"'Son of Atreus, was this after all the better way for both, for you and me, that we, for all our hearts' sorrow, quarrelled together for the sake of a girl in soul-perishing hatred? I wish Artemis had killed her beside the ships with an arrow on that day when I destroyed Lyrnessos and took her. For thus not all these too many Achaians would have bitten the dust, by enemy hands, when I was away in my anger. This way was better for the Trojans and Hektor; yet I think the Achaians will too long remember this quarrel between us. Still, we will let all this be a thing of the past, though it hurts us, and beat down by constraint the anger that rises inside us. Now I am making an end of my anger. It does not become me unrelentingly to rage on.'" — Achilles, *Iliad* 19:56

You are out with some friends, celebrating a done deal. You go from bar to bar, slipping money to bouncers. Everywhere is hot and crowded and smoky. Everywhere is loud with music and shouting and decor. Everywhere there are pretty girls in miniskirts or backless shirts or cutoff tops but the prettiest ones are always the ones serving you — the bartenders, the waitresses, the hostesses.

And after a while, after you've all had more than a few drinks, after more than a few of you have gone home, one of your friends says, "Hey — we're right around the corner from my new place, you guys wanna come up and see?" And it seems like a good idea so you all go upstairs.

And his girlfriend opens the door, a girl only a couple of you have met and even then only once or twice. She's not angry, he must have told her he'd be out late, she just decided to wait up for him. "Hey guys," she says sweetly. She's wearing blue jeans and a T-shirt and no shoes. Not something she'd wear out but not something that looks terrible either. She doesn't have any makeup on, her hair is pulled back in a ponytail. She still looks pretty though, just not that pretty — the light in his apartment is not dimmed or neon.

"You look fat," he says, as he walks in. But you all ignore him and his comment as you scatter to look around, see the view, the kitchen, the media setup. You all know he's just showing off.

Preferring to be near people who speak their language, the great majority of army veterans live within ten miles of an army base. We can use this information to derive a divorce rate for veterans by looking at the divorce rates in the counties in which army bases are located.

When we do so we discover that these rates are more or less the same as the national average. Which should make us wonder not why the divorce rate for veterans is not higher than the national average, but why the divorce rate for civilians is as high as that for veterans.

You said it when your hands had long since ceased to ever smell of ground coffee or chopped garlic. You said it as we returned from the mountains.

We had taken the small gauge rail high up to a village where you had somehow heard all the locals bought their chests. It was a tiny place, ten houses or so with eaves that reached to the ground because of the snow. But there was no snow when we were there.

It was a warm summer day and displayed outside were dozens of wooden chests. They were beautiful, hand-painted with folkloric designs of reindeer and men and women in traditional clothing, hand-painted in reds and greens and whites. We bought half of them. You were thinking of opening a shop.

Then, as we boarded the train, as the sun began to set, you said, "This is what you want, you know, somewhere completely unspoiled."

Or perhaps it wasn't the mountains. Perhaps it was the coast and the carpenters were fishermen. Perhaps the chests were nets hung from the cliffs to dry. Perhaps you weren't even thinking of opening a shop. But that was what you said. And that was when you said it.

After the *Iliad*, the *Odyssey* is inevitable. And it should come as no surprise that artful Odysseus survives while mighty Achilles does not.

And so if we are watching our son or daughter at a swim meet, with that chlorine smell and dampness and haze in the air, with that fear of slipping as we walk to our seats or to get a soda from a vending machine, and they beat their own personal best time in their event but they still come in last, we give them a hug. We say, as they stand there and shiver with a towel around them, with their wet hair disheveled from the cap, as they look at the winners receiving their medals, we say, "Don't worry about it, you beat your best time, right? You should be proud of yourself — what more could you have done?"

And they say, "I know, I know."

Because they do. They know it doesn't matter if they are fast, only if they are faster. They know virtues are virtuous only by comparison. They know if they are fast but everyone else is faster, they are slow. They know if they are fast but everyone else is faster, they come in last. They lose. They know if they'd been faster and not just fast we would have said, "Way to go! You won! That was great!" and taken them out for a special dinner where there'd be laughter and one of their friends or even the whole team.

And if they don't know this, if they weren't in the swim meet or the science bowl or the battle of the bands, if they weren't somehow competing to begin with, we know it's our job to teach it to them.

So they can never give us what those young girls we fuck do. Because they are our daughters, not someone else's. It is not enough that they are beautiful. It is not enough that they like to have fun. It is not enough that they are alive, but that they survive.

And this is why we feel like failures as parents if we see that our children don't think they have anything to prove. Why when they say not, "I want to be a professional surfer," but simply, "I want to surf," even the most understanding of us — even sometimes those of us with enough money that we don't have to worry about them making a living — why we look at them and wonder, just for a second, how this thing that came out of us could be so unlike us, so far away from us, wonder, just for a second, if they are, in fact, ours.

This is why, if we are good parents, we teach them to swim as soon as possible. We teach them for their own good. We teach them even though we know it is in keeping our heads above water that we drown.

And yet not all vampires are men, far from it. In fact after Vlad the Impaler the next most classic model for the modern vampire legend is the sixteenth-century Hungarian countess Erzsébet Bathory. She believed that human blood could maintain the skin in a state of "youthful perfection." So she had peasants brought to her boudoir where they were killed and had the blood drained from their bodies. Then, while it was still fresh and warm (naturally, since, if kept for any period of time, it would have coagulated), the countess would bathe in it. For this purpose, before she was brought to trial and executed, she had six hundred and thirteen people murdered.

However, not just any peasant would do. According to the countess the only blood capable of performing this miracle was that of teenage girls.

There is that one incident you've never talked about with anyone even though everyone knows about it, even though every now and then you still overhear people gossiping about it, people new enough they don't think to check the stalls before they gossip about the CEO the day he's visiting their office.

You've never talked about it with anyone even though it happened, what, ten, fifteen years ago? More? Less? In fact, no one's even tried to talk to you about it since the night your wife found out and she said, "Do you want to talk about it?" and you said, "No," and she said, "OK, well let me know if you do." Sometimes you wonder what would happen if you called her up now, in Oregon or Hong Kong or wherever she lives now, and said, "OK. Now. Now I want to talk about it."

You wonder that when you can't help thinking about it. When it is late and you are alone. When the other people on your plane are asleep and the blinds are down and all you can hear is the faint noise of the jets, faint because it's a very expensive plane, and you only stop thinking about it because your stewardess says quietly, "Can I get you another one?" When because it is a nice night and you haven't walked in a while you dismiss your driver after dinner and tell him you're going to walk the thirty-four blocks home. When you cut your hand on the coral almost right away and have to come up so it's just you and the captain and the mate on the boat while everyone else is still down there and the mate comes over to you with some gauze as you stare down into the water at the reef just ten or twenty feet below and says, "It's too bad you can't see her, she's a beaut. . . ."

When you think how he said, "I'm going to fight you on this." The man you'd known for years, the man you started the damn company with in the first place, the man you couldn't have done it without, the man who knew how to push those Turks around the way they needed to be pushed around to get your export taxes low enough, the man who held down the fort those five months Jillian was sick, the man who realized the key benefit wasn't actually what everyone, even the consultants, thought it was.

When you think how you said, "OK, but you'll lose, I already persuaded the board," and he said, "We'll see," and he put up a really good fight, found some really great lawyer with a Bombay accent, but he lost anyway because all that really mattered in the end was that the judge, some stern and haughty bitch with eyes like blue slate or grey sky, wanted in on the IPO of a company spun off by a guy who owed you and only you a favor.

When you think how when she announced her decision, he actually stood up and said, "Goddamn it! You fucking bitch!" and actually threw his table over, actually had to be restrained by three bailiffs, how even though he was one of the largest men you'd ever seen, it didn't matter in the end.

When you think how long it took for the news to reach you, how you didn't hear for more than five days, how when you did hear, the first thing you thought was, "I wonder where he got a gun?" How when you did hear, even though you felt bad, you refused to feel guilty. How you still tell yourself you did the right thing, the only thing, a thing you'd do again if it was as necessary. How you still tell yourself you're not a bad man, just a man who sees things clearly.

When you think how you've never talked about it with anyone because the one person you could have talked about it with, the one person you wouldn't have had to talk about it with, is the one person you couldn't talk to now even if you wanted to.

And yet it was to avenge his companion Patroclus that Achilles finally entered the battle.

And yet, in the end, it was not glorious Hector, but craven Paris who killed him.

You have been walking the crowded streets of Cairo, eating a handful of dates one at a time, looking for quality rugs. You have been riding horses in the Andes and come into a village for a lunch of fried guinea pig, *papas fritas*, and Fanta. At dawn, a Sherpa has been slowly driving you out of town in an open Jeep to head up to the monastery in the mountains. You have left a meeting in Tokyo and been stepping into your limousine.

In all these places a pair of teenage girls has walked past wearing less than they should be. In all of these places you have turned your head to follow them. In all of these places you have looked up from them and met the eyes of another man. And in all of these places you have smiled at each other with absolute understanding. In all of these places it has been this that you could share with other men.

In the chariot race in the *Iliad*, Eumelus says nothing about his bad luck, it is Achilles that takes pity on him of his own free will. But in the *Aeneid*, Eumelus' analog complains that he was robbed by fortune and deserves a prize anyway, which he gets.

Likewise in the *Iliad*, Menelaus says he will take care of Antilochus' cheating himself and Antilochus, afraid of Menelaus, immediately gives him the prize he won unfairly. But in the *Aeneid*, when the opponent of Antilochus' analog complains of cheating, that opponent is given a special prize because of his complaint, allowing Antilochus' analog to keep the prize he won unfairly.

Back when we only had one car you had to drop me off at my job on the way to your job. And everyday you would kiss me good-bye at the same stoplight two blocks away from my building. You knew you couldn't kiss me as I got out of the car. Someone might have seen.

The earliest known use of the word "cunt" in its modern form and meaning is in 1230 A.D. In that year it appeared in Ekwall's *Street Names of the City of London* as part of the name "Grope Cunt Lane." It is not difficult to imagine what trade was plied there.

The origin of the word, however, is something of a mystery. Prior to this use it appears only in Medieval Latin in the form *kunte,* which has led some scholars to speculate it came into the language from Old Norse since it resembles an Old Norse word in form. However, there is no equivalent to the word in Old Norse.

It therefore seems much more likely that the word is a Norsification of the Latin word *cunnus,* meaning "female reproductive organ" (the Latin word *vagina,* which we adopted as a euphemism for the unmentionable *cunnus,* actually meant "sheath for a weapon").

The origin of this word is not in doubt nor particularly interesting. It comes from the Greek word *kuo* of the same meaning.

However, once we realize this, what does become interesting is Homer's coining of the term *kunopis* or "dog-faced." He uses this term only in reference to women, to Helen in particular but also to others, both gods and mortals, and it is clear from later usage that the term was intended to imply shameless, reprehensible, deceitful behavior. What is interesting about his use of this word is that it is compounded from the female form of the word for "dog," *kuon. Kunopis* was a pun. It meant "with a face like a dog" but it would also make listeners think of the female reproductive organ. As a "writer," he could not have chosen a more perfect word.

But he also could not have foreseen that so long after his death, because his work had become so familiar to both the later Greeks and the Romans after them, this whimsical association he had made would carry on. So it was that even after the word *kuo* had become *cunnus* in Latin and the word *kuon* had become *canis*, even after it was no longer a pun, Latin authors still referred to women as "dog-faced."

And once we understand this, we can solve another supposed etymological mystery. The derivation of the word "cunning."

Again, it is speculated that this word comes from Nordic roots, in this case from the Anglo-Saxon verb "to know," *kunnan*, and again this seems unlikely. After all, the vixen knows nothing but is no less cunning for her ignorance.

So we look more closely and what do we find? That in Old English, "cunning" meant "to have had sex with," as in "I had cunning of her." And that the first recorded usage of the word "cunning" in English occurs in 1325 in *The Proverbs of Hending* where it is used in the epigram, "Directly equal is the cunt to cunning . . ." When we look more closely we find that once again the more likely parental candidate is *cunnus*.

And is it really so hard to imagine the origin of the words "cunt" and "cunning" is one and the same? Words that appeared in English usage at a time when anyone literate would have become so by reading the classics in Latin? Is it so far-fetched to believe both words are derived ultimately from the word *kuo* and its Homeric associations? The one meaning the internal female genitalia; the other meaning sly, crafty, skillful in deception?

And perhaps this would be less credible if not for the fact that at the time of the appearance of both of these words, at the time when the shift was being made from written Latin to written English, there is evidence that the word "dog" maintained its associations with cowardliness and worthlessness (1325 A.D., *Coer de Leon*). Perhaps this would be less credible if we did not have this evidence that in the thirteenth and early-fourteenth centuries A.D., "dog" still carried the same implications it did to Homer, possibly because of Homer.

And perhaps this would be less credible if not for the fact that today we still use "dog" to mean both "ugly woman" and "something that performs below expectations," if not for the fact that we still use "bitch" when, supposedly unaware of the redundancy, we mean "cunning cunt."

And perhaps this would be less credible if not for the fact that the word "pussy" (as an alternative to "cunt") was first coined not only by a woman, but also at the beginning of the women's suffrage movement. Perhaps this would be less credible if not for the fact that so many women dislike the word "cunt," if not for the fact that so many women prefer the word "pussy" but never seem to know why. Perhaps this would be less credible if not for the fact that after 3,000 years without a voice, the word women have spoken for themselves means "cat" and not "dog."

You have one friend that's a woman. You've known her for years. For a long time she was your enemy — you were in engineering, she was in marketing. You used to go home sometimes and your wife would just have to look at you to know "that fucking bitch" had done something else.

But then you both left and started your own companies and almost forgot about each other until you bumped into each other at the Four Cats in Barcelona.

You were eating alone at one of the tables on the balcony or the mezzanine or whatever they called it in Cataluña, looking down through the railings, and you saw her come in. And you watched her sit down by herself and you finished your bisque but no one joined her so in between courses you went downstairs and walked up to her table and said, "This is a coincidence."

But it turned out it wasn't. After she eyed you suspiciously and you dispensed with formalities about health and marital status and children you discovered you were both there to give a bid to the same company, a company that had told you both they weren't looking at anyone else yet. And she said "son of a bitch" and you said "motherfucker" and you had them bring the rest of your meal to her table and you noticed you were attracted to her even though by now she had to be at least fifteen years older than the girl you fucked the night before you left New York, you noticed that, in fact, you had been attracted to her all those years before but had never wanted to admit it could be anything more than a "hate fuck."

And you talked and compared scars and apologized to each other, both said you hadn't understood where the other was coming from back then but that now you did because you'd both had to deal with problems from all the departments. And you would have shared a bottle or two of wine except that you drank scotch and she drank vodka.

And afterwards you didn't bother to exchange cards because you'd known how to reach each other all these years if you'd wanted to and you walked out to your cars and as the crisp night air hit the two of you, you restored the conversation to its appropriate formality now that you were departing, you asked, "So where are you staying?"

And after she told you she looked at you and said, "What? . . . What?"

And you said, "Those idiots — they recommended the same place to me — that's where I'm staying!"

And she said, "You're kidding!" and you both laughed when you were supposed to be saying, "Good luck — maybe I'll see you in the City sometime." And when you were done laughing for some reason you looked at each other like a couple of high school kids on a doorstep and there was a pause and for some reason you leaned in to kiss her and she didn't stop you but she didn't respond either but then her lips began to purse but then she pulled back and said, "No, no — bad idea."

And you weren't even disappointed, you just stood up again and shrugged and said, "Yeah, you're right." And you said good-bye and as you walked over to your car you said, "Good luck — maybe I'll see you in the City sometime," and she said, "Maybe — you too," but then before either of you got in your cars she said, "You know we might as well share a car." And you said, "Yeah, I guess you're right" and then you both looked at each other for a moment waiting for the other to come over but in the end it was her that dismissed her driver. And on the ride back to the hotel neither of you said anything, you had said all there was to say for just then.

But when you fucked it was no good. It took you a long time to come and you weren't sure if she came at all. She was still in great shape, her skin was still smooth for the most part, you really only thought about her age when you saw her hand around your cock. And it wasn't for lack of skill, when she blew you she looked at you as she deep-throated you, caressed that spot just behind your balls, had long trails of saliva running from her mouth to your cock. It was that you both produced condoms and you wore the one from the box you had, not the one from the little metal case in her purse. It was that when you pulled out of her from behind and tried to turn her over on her back, her hip pushed back against your hand and she said, "Don't stop." It was that she thought she was fucking you and you thought you were fucking her.

And then, after she left your room to go back to hers to sleep, you didn't see her or hear from her until you called her office on a whim a few months later and played phone tag with her for a couple weeks and eventually had dinner on the Upper East Side. And at first neither of you was sure why the other had come but you were the one who had made the first call so it was up to you to make the crack about your "unsuccessful merger" as soon as possible and then you both knew why you were there and suddenly had plenty to say and had a perfectly pleasant dinner that ended with you accepting her invitation to "bring someone" down to her restored deco penthouse in South Beach over Labor Day.

And that weekend turned out to be a lot of fun because right after you arrived the girl you had brought said she wanted to get a new swimsuit right away but you didn't feel like going because you wanted to have a drink first so your host said her boyfriend wouldn't mind showing your girlfriend where to go and the two of you sent the two of them off and as soon as the door closed you had looked at her with one eyebrow raised and said, "Enrique?!" and she had looked at you the same way at the same time and said, "Tiffany?!" and then you both laughed although this time it wasn't like a couple of high school kids on a doorstep. That weekend turned out to be a lot of fun because when you went out to dinner and the waitstaff assumed the two of you were married and that Tiffany was your daughter and therefore, because of his skin color, Enrique was her boyfriend, you both thought that was funny too although if you hadn't both had someone to share it with it would have irritated either of you. That weekend turned out to be a lot of fun because Sunday night when she said to you, "I think Enrique fucked Tiffany this afternoon when we left them alone," you said, "I don't care, do you?" and she said, "No, I don't care — I thought you might."

And after that you saw her as much as you saw anyone and you learned as much about her as you learned about anyone. You learned that she dates as many young boys as you do young girls although she'd never let them dress her, or read anything they recommended, or let them decide where they were going for the weekend. You learned that even though she dates as many young boys as you do young girls, she wouldn't consider marrying any of them any more than she'd consider marrying her scuba gear or her favorite squash racket or any other toy. You learned that when they ask her for something she says, "Maybe," not, "Of course." You learned that when she calls an escort service she also specifies that they be as young as possible but that for her it is nothing more than an aesthetic choice, she simply prefers having sex with younger men or, as she puts it, "If I'm going to drive a car just for the pleasure of driving a car, that car better be mint. . . ." You learned that when she wants to indulge herself, she takes mineral salt baths, she treats herself to a day spa. You learned that "pampering" herself makes her feel "100 percent better," "reborn," "like a new woman," "like she can breathe again."

And if you continue to remain friends, if you manage to avoid butting heads over a client at some point, if you can avoid stabbing each other in the back (an event which has always seemed inevitable enough that while you tell each other what you do you never tell each other what you want), if you can do that for long enough maybe eventually you will learn that those times when there's no one else in your house or apartment and you say "thank God," and pour yourself a scotch and sit in the media room and watch a DVD, those times are the same times she sits in her empty dining room and forces herself not to cry.

All's fair in love and war.

You know what time the high schools let out. It's not something you researched, you didn't look it up or wait outside one all day long. You just happened to be passing one one day as it was letting out and you happened to notice the time. You don't make special visits. You don't go out of your way. But if you are passing by, you do check the time. Just to see if you should linger a moment or two.

Immortal Poseidon, God of the Sea, God of the Earthquake, God of Fast Cars.

Royal Odysseus, Man of Twists and Turns, Formula One Engineer.

Alexander, Caesar, de' Medici, Richelieu, Napoleon, Victoria. Although it would be too unpopular to admit, these are our real heroes, the ones who did what they needed to do to get what they wanted. Not the peacemakers, not the meek.

Although we could never mention it as anything but a joke, Genghis Khan's saying "The three great pleasures in life are: to crush your enemies, to ride their horses, and to take their women to bed" is one of our favorites.

And even though we do confess that we love that bit in *The*

Godfather when Michael Corleone says, "Don't ever ask me about my business," even though we may openly claim we prefer Grendel to Beowulf, Vader to Skywalker (and yet not Paris to Hector nor Hector to Achilles), we can only do so in these cases because they are fictional.

Although it would be too unpopular to admit, we don't wish we could be ruthless, we wish we could get away with being ruthless.

You once read that vinyl dissolved in seawater.

You once read that too much fish oil could be toxic.

You once read that your face would stay that way.

But later, one way or another, you learned that none of these things were true. They were just devices. They were just fiction. They just made a good story better.

I saw you by so many columns and arches, I saw you in so many sacred places.

In Cuzco, the leopard-shaped city, you ran your hand over a wall. You wore no rings, not one, not yet. "It's so smooth," you said. "Even where the blocks meet, it's so smooth it's amazing." The guidebook said that before the Spanish came it had been sheathed in gold. As we walked away, as we walked towards a stand that sold yellow Inca Kola in glass bottles, you said, "It must have been very beautiful before the conquest."

And I said something about the sacrificial victims probably not agreeing with you and you laughed. "Very funny," you said. This was when I still said things to make you laugh and you still laughed at things I said. We bought some soda and you tossed your hair back and threw your head back and you drank. Even though the bottle had been reused so many times, even though its ridges and buttons were worn away, it still winked in the sun.

In Paris we looked at the shape of Notre-Dame. Recently damaged by a violent windstorm, its exterior was hidden by metal frames and blue tarpaulin that snapped and cracked in the breeze. You held your hand up to your forehead to block the sun from your squinting eyes. By then you wore jewelry. "That's a shame," you said. "Still, we can always catch it next time." Even though we could see our breath, you suggested we cross the bridge to Île Saint-Louis and buy some gelato at that place where you said you'd heard everyone went for gelato.

In Amarna you made me stand still for scale. You walked far, far away and you took a picture. It was of three temples stacked like bricks. An excavation around a mosque had revealed it was built on the roof of a Roman church in turn built on the roof of an Egyptian temple. I came out as a tiny red dot.

In Petra you said, "This is what I wanted to see." You were looking up at the capitals of the columns of the great temple. They had only recently been reconstructed. On their corners, they had elephant heads. "These are the only elephant-headed columns in the world," you said. "None of our friends have seen anything like this." That night we slept in tents but had Bedouins to bring us dates and figs.

On Easter Island we spent the day walking among the supplicant *moai*, their eyes scattered or missing altogether. There was one wall there they thought had been somehow built by an Inca and you had me take a picture of you in front of it. Then, years later, you came to me with it in your hand as I reviewed some process flowcharts and said, "Hey — look at this, that's weird, one of the pictures from Peru got in with the batch from Easter Island!" And I looked at the picture and I said, "No, that was from Easter Island — that one wall, remember? The one they think was somehow built by an Inca? Besides — look how old you are there. You were much younger in Peru." And then you looked at the picture more closely and said, "Oh, I think you're right — now I remember."

In Kenya it was Kilimanjaro; in Turkey, Ararat; in Japan, Fuji. In Greece it was Olympus I saw you on the slopes of.

Eventually, you said, "Everything is sacred, isn't it?" By then I couldn't have disagreed more.

The brilliance of the name Odysseus is that it can mean either giver or receiver of pain.

You are at a cocktail party a friend of yours is having, a small, informal affair, just a few people. And he introduces you to a man and his boyfriend. The man is your age, the boyfriend in his late teens, early twenties. The three of you chat for a while, you and the older man are in the same field, get along well. Eventually the boyfriend goes to get more hors d'oeuvres. And when he walks off you say with a smirk, "How old is he, anyway?"

And the other man looks at you and grins and glances at the floor, at the wall, anywhere he can avoid your eyes, and then looks up at you and squints and bites his bottom lip as if he's in pain and says, "Nineteen." And you chuckle and shake your head and wag your finger and he raises his eyebrows and nods his head. And it is then, as — still smiling — you both take sips of your drinks, you realize it doesn't matter if someone's gay.

Why did you decide ceasing to tolerate our lovers was a better course of action than simply taking your own?

She takes you to a concert at a nightclub. It is loud. Concerts were loud when you had the time to go to them more often, your ears would still ring the next morning, but not like this. Here, they hit certain chords that resonate with your skull, with your inner ear, certain distorted chords that make you lose your sense of balance. And you are not alone in this, you can see everyone become dizzy when they play one of those chords. Everyone begins to reel, this has nothing to do with the fact that you are one of only about seven men there over thirty, one of only about seven men there with girls half their age or less.

The band plays electronic dance music with a pounding, driving beat. The lead singer, probably just a front, is a woman in her late twenties. Although not especially pretty, she is far from ugly and is tremendously appealing because she seems so slutty. As the show goes on, she changes outfits constantly, one thing more revealing than the next, and as she performs she humps a chair, squats near the front of the stage with her legs spread wide open, rubs the microphone cord back and forth between her legs. And there is also an S&M stage show, a variety of things. A man is wheeled out hanging by handcuffs from a metal bar and she whips him while she performs. Two girls are brought out in metal bustiers, chained to crosses and have circular saws applied to their breasts by men dressed as butchers, their faces hidden in leather masks. The saws send arcs of brilliant white sparks out into the audience.

You feel a little awkward, you never liked to dance very much unless you were really drunk. You've never felt so self-conscious about your baldness. For the third or fourth number they play a song you know from college, from when this kind of music was new, from only — what? — fifteen, sixteen years ago? They announce it as a "classic."

While the band and the crowd warm up, you find yourself scanning the room, looking for girls who didn't qualify for a wrist-band. When you find one, you examine her. So much exposed flesh here, so many of those stomachs with pierced belly buttons, stomachs that would hang if the girls weren't sucking them in but that still look appetizing because even though they're not muscled, even though they're chubby — but not flabby, not yet — even though they have no waist, they don't need any of those things. You tremble when you look at those bellies and their boyfriends' hands crawl across them. You find you are staring at girls that you would never look at if they were closer to your age, never look at if they were in their late twenties even, girls you and your friends would make fun of among yourselves if they were just slightly older and you saw them on the street dressed the same way — cutoff leather halter tops, exposed garter belts, rubber spiked dog collars, latex evening gloves.

One girl who can't be more than thirteen wears a shirt that says BEAT ME, FUCK ME, EAT ME, WHIP ME, CUM ON MY TITS, AND THEN GET THE FUCK OUT! The first thing that comes to mind is, "What tits?" and only then do you wonder how she got in here, why a girl that young would be wearing a shirt like that.

"Can you get me a drink?" the girl who brought you here shouts. You nod, push your way through the crowd to the bar. You only hear questions like that when you're out with girls her age. And it's not because they're too young to buy alcohol for themselves, which they are. It's because they are the only ones who aren't constantly trying to figure out what they can do for you. Because they are the only ones who aren't afraid of you. Because they are the only ones who don't yet have anything to lose.

At the point where you manage to squeeze up to the bar, there is a pretty girl leaning against it watching the stage, her elbows resting on the wooden lip behind her. Her hair is dyed black, her lips painted dark red, her face powdered white, her eyes heavily kohled. She has a metal stud below her lower lip. She wears a PVC bodysuit that ends in gloves and four-inch stiletto heels. She has it unzipped to just below her sternum but it is so tight on her she is in no danger of exposing anything more than the inner side of each breast. This is more than enough to set your heart pounding. You wonder if she could actually zip the suit up any more even if she wanted to. You also notice she isn't wearing a wristband. You make eye contact and raise your eyebrows, purse your lips in a smile. Her only reaction is to look away.

As you wait for the bartender, facing the opposite direction to her, you can't help yourself. You have to glance down her front more than once. The bartender comes over to you quickly, ignoring several people that have been waiting longer than you, people that are younger than you, people not as bald as you.

As you order you take out your ostrich-skin Gucci wallet. What you order makes the girl glance over her shoulder at you, at your wallet. She turns around. Leans on the bar by bending at the waist instead of slumping her back. You glance at her ass, thrust out into the crowd, the colored lights forming shining bands on the glistening rubber, bands that follow the curve of her body. Every man that walks past looks at this part of her. Most, coming across her in the middle of the dense crowd, look surprised. Their heavy eyes widen, they throw their heads back a little, their eyebrows raise. It is almost as if they narrowly avoided stepping on a snake in dense brush. Almost, but not quite. There is no fear. With one exception, the men that don't react are with women. They look, but it is a quick glance, nothing more. The exception is the youngest, a junior high kid. The girl he is with, heavily made up but probably about twelve, punches him in the ribs.

"Awesome, huh?" the girl in the bodysuit shouts at you.

"Yeah, awesome!" you shout back, nodding, watching the bartender. He brings your drinks, says, "That'll be twenty-seven fifty."

When you open your wallet, the girl glances in. It is a quick look, subtle, but you catch it anyway. When you take your change, she looks one more time, thinking you can't see her do it out of the corner of your eye. If you weren't already here with someone, with a girl calling herself an "aspiring model," a girl a friend of yours who runs an agency set you up with . . .

You pick up the two drinks, and, taking a sip from yours, nod at her. She nods back, starts to say something, but is cut off by a guy in his early twenties who forces his way between the two of you.

As you walk off, you hear him order three drinks, hear the bartender tell him that for three drinks he needs three wristbands. As you walk off, you wonder why he didn't say something similar to you.

And you know she watched you walk away, cursed because the guy cut her off. Later you see her near you in the crowd, see her examine the young blonde you are with, the young blonde that reeks of old New York City wealth even in her motorcycle jacket and temporary tattoo. Later you see her walk away.

As you walk back, a group of six girls comes out onstage. They are all dressed to hide only what it is absolutely necessary to hide. One Asian girl in pigtails and high heels wears nothing more than a single band of black electrical tape around her chest and three or four bands around her hips. The group begins a number with only one lyric: "I wanna see your pussy, show it to me!" Somehow changed into a micro-mini rubber dress, the singer shouts this out and does various things to the girls — bends them over and spanks them, leads them around on all fours by leashes, sticks her hand up their skirts.

The show excites you, makes you bold. You hand the girl her drink which she takes with two hands, careful not to spill any, smiling a thank-you at you — a genuine thank-you, an unobligated thank-you. Then you slip your free hand around her waist, place it on the spot below her waist where she will begin to swell over the next few years, pull her back towards you. She doesn't stop you, doesn't even seem to notice she is so mesmerized by the stage. You, on the other hand, have lost interest in the lesbian act, something that would have held your attention for hours if you had been here with men and only men. Now you are concentrating on her tiny, hard ass pushed into your crotch, on the feel of it on either side of your cock. You can't help worrying slightly. You don't want to get too much of an erection but you also don't want to seem too small, too flaccid. You're not even sure if she's aware of the contact. But she must be.

When the song is done she leans her head back and gives you a peck on the lips. Then, completely at ease, she slips her free hand around the back of your leg, holds you tight to her.

The singer has changed outfits again. Now she wears a purple velvet catsuit with stiletto ankle boots. Over it she wears a kind of rubber harness that supports a line of giant metal spikes that run along her spine. The ones in the middle stick out more than a foot.

She walks up to the edge of the stage. She is dripping with sweat. Leaning down to the front row she says, "Are there any young boys here tonight?" A range of kids in the front row go crazy. She picks out two of them and invites them up on the stage. One is scrawny, about fourteen or fifteen with purple hair. The other is better muscled, a little older, possibly a little Asian, but still by no means a man. As the song starts she makes a motion to pull their shirts off. With no more prompting than that, the boys help her, rip their shirts off over their heads and throw them to the audience.

She starts singing. "something something something YOUNG BOYS something something something!" You are not alone, you are not the only one who can't make out anything but those two words. But those two words are all you need to make out to know what the song is about. Perhaps those two words are the only two words you're supposed to understand.

And then you notice the strangest thing. This is really turning you on. This is the highlight of the show. You're not bi (no, you're really not, you've thought about it — perhaps even tried it — it's not that it disgusts you, it just doesn't excite you), it has nothing to do with that. It's just exciting you in a way the fake lesbian show never could. It excites you tremendously to see that woman up there groping these young boys, clutching at them, grabbing their hair and pushing them onto their knees and shoving their faces in her gyrating crotch as she sings.

They love it, of course. They are a little awkward, a little self-conscious, but they still grind up next to her, on either side of her, even there and then are already wondering if she'll take them backstage after the show and fuck them, even there and then are already thinking about what their friends are going to say, about how they'll tell the ones that weren't here about this. They would love to be used by her.

And it isn't just you. You look around for the other men your age and they too are mesmerized, they too have stopped pawing the girls that brought them here. And it is not just them, the entire crowd is going crazy, wilder than they have yet. Even though they're so young, they still recognize this is a special ritual. Even though they're so young, they still recognize this is something unique. It reminds you of a long and bloody boxing match between a popular champion and an unpopular challenger, a long and bloody boxing match where the challenger at last grows woozy in the final round, at last begins to stumble, and the crowd begins to shout with one voice, "Finish him." A long and bloody boxing match where, by the end, even the women are shouting for blood. It is just like that. You and everyone there wants to see her gorge herself on those two boys, satiate herself with them, pleasure herself with them, use them. If she had men up there with her, handsome men with perfect bodies but men, people closer to her own age or a little older, it wouldn't be the same thing. Even if she actually stripped down naked and fucked them right there on the stage as she sang, it wouldn't be the same thing. You certainly wouldn't be interested, would turn your attention to groping the young girl you are with. And the rest of the crowd, while they might be young enough to still be excited by that kind of display, they wouldn't be excited in the same way, to the same degree. They would know it just wasn't the same thing.

This turns out to be their final number, this is what this band chose for their finale.

As you file out with the crowd, as the aspiring model pulls your head down to her and says quietly in your ear, "I don't have to be home until two," you consider how different it would have been if the singer had been a man. About how if it was a man up there and he pulled two high school freshman girls out of the audience and pushed them onto their knees and shoved their heads to his crotch, the two cops near the door would have stopped the show. About how, for some reason, that would have been public indecency.

Then again, you think as the cold night air hits your face, a man wouldn't have worn those spikes down his back. A man wouldn't have been afraid of the strange girls getting behind him, of them doing something he couldn't see. If it was a man up there with two underage girls, he wouldn't have been worried about that, he wouldn't have been worried about losing control.

"Then resourceful Odysseus spoke in turn and answered her: 'Goddess and queen, do not be angry with me. I myself know that all you say is true and that circumspect Penelope can never match the impression you make for beauty and stature. She is mortal after all, and you are immortal and ageless.'"
— *Odyssey* 5:214

The wildest friend, the one you once saw walk up to a boy of about five or six who'd been left alone for a minute and say, "Did you know your mom's fucking hot?" that one, that friend. He's always the one who falls the hardest. He's always the one who disappears the most completely when he finds a woman that will put up with him.

After the collapse of the Russian economy, wealthy men began to travel to Moscow for one reason nobody expected. The prostitution.

It wasn't that the Russian prostitutes at that time were particularly young or particularly beautiful or particularly skilled. It also wasn't because there were so many to choose from at a time when three out of four adolescent Muscovite girls said they aspired to be prostitutes. It was because literally thousands of women who had been previously employed in jobs requiring high levels of training and intelligence were suddenly forced to turn to prostitution to survive, a unique situation due to the combination of the rapidity of the economic shift with the time and place at which it occurred.

As a result, everyone discovered this quality was just as marketable as youth or beauty or skill, perhaps even more so. A plain, thirty-four-year-old, former heart surgeon, for example, would find that her blowjobs were worth the same as those of a beautiful, nineteen-year-old former bus driver.

It was this experience, available nowhere else in the world, that was apparently worth a special trip to Moscow for so many wealthy men, the experience of paying a woman with a Ph.D. to let you blindfold her, tie her hands behind her back, and cum in her mouth.

But how did the men know they were getting what they'd paid for? What proofs were offered, what guarantees? What was the equivalent of the chicken bladder full of blood placed in the cervix of the pubescent teen sold for the twenty-third time as a virgin? Were there academic credentials forged for this purpose and this purpose alone? What if all the women claiming to be former international lawyers were impostors? What if there were no architects forced to become whores?

And when we bought a second place, an apartment in the city, you decorated it yourself and you said to me, "You have to see it, it looks great — when are you coming home?"

The word "work" is derived from the Middle English *werk.* This in turn comes from the Anglo-Saxon *werc,* which, it is thought, is an adaptation of the Indo-European base *werg* from the Greek *ergon.* This word was used in all the same ways we use "work" today but also applied to one additional situation. *Ergon* was also used to refer to what men did in battle.

Likewise our modern word "charm" comes from the Latin for song, incantation, or inscription, *carmen,* which was taken in turn from the Greek *charma* meaning "source of joy." *Charma* gave the Greeks all the words one would expect, like, for example, their word for "rejoice," *chairo.* But it was also from this word that the Greeks derived the word *charme.* In modern English *charme* best translates as "combat."

All of which makes one wonder — no matter how impossible it may seem in a time when ancient Greek was lost — if Shakespeare was aware of this when he had Macbeth, shortly before he is killed by Macduff, coin the term "charmed life."

And so we want faster cars, faster boats, faster jets, faster computers — anything more powerful than everything else. And we continue to want them even after we learn that there's nowhere worth going except where we left and that the faster we go, the further away from there we get.

You might have had a dog once. You might have liked him a lot. And he probably liked you even more. You might have played with him every day. You might have taught him all kinds of commands. He might have made you smile whenever you came home no matter how shitty your life was. He really might have been willing to die for you without hesitation.

But sometimes when you fed him, you couldn't help thinking that maybe this was what your whole relationship was based on. That if somehow he decided where and when and what you ate, you would be the one sleeping on the floor, the one balancing the bone on your nose until he said, "OK," the one sitting up on your haunches when he said, "Beg."

If you had a dog once, sometimes this was something you couldn't help thinking.

You will be staying with an old friend after your second divorce. It will be night, cloudless, moonless, you will be at his house in the country down by his boathouse. You will be sitting out on his pier hanging your legs over the edge, drinking beer from the bottle. It won't be cheap beer but it will still come in bottles. You will be like a couple of boys but for the fact that somewhere in the back of both your minds you will be vaguely worried you might lose a shoe to the lake, might get some kind of stain on the seat of your pants. There really will be a blanket of stars.

You will have been discussing work, there will be a silence. There really will be crickets and the odd bullfrog, the odd splashing noise from somewhere out on the lake. "Bill," you will say, "how have you done it? How have you managed to stay with Karen? I mean, you've been married since you were twenty for Christ's sakes!"

There will be another pause. "She likes eighteen-year-old blondes," Bill will say at last.

You will laugh. He's kidding. "You're kidding," you will say. But then you will look at him and you will see he's not kidding. He's not smiling, he's just looking out over the lake. He will take a sip from his beer.

"Come on! Really?! Karen?" Even in your surprise you will manage to find space to imagine Bill's wife finger fucking a younger girl. Karen will still be very attractive. "What about trust? What about being honest with each other? Aren't you supposed to say something about that?"

"Oh there's all of that too," Bill will say, drinking again, "you have to have that too — you have to be completely honest with each other from day one — that's why she's comfortable with us sharing someone — that's why she's not threatened, she's known who I was from the beginning — Christ, on our very first date we ended up talking about strip clubs somehow — I think she was comparing bridal showers to bachelor parties or something — and she asked me if I liked them. I said, 'yes,' and told her why. And she was fine with it. If she hadn't been there wouldn't have been a second date. And if I'd lied to her, told her what I thought she'd want to hear, then there shouldn't have been a second date. Every lie you tell, the next one comes a little easier." He will look at you then and you must seem surprised, like you've just been told that, in fact, there is a Santa Claus, because he will add, "Look — I'm not saying we wouldn't have lasted this long without that, I'd like to think we would have and still without cheating on each other, but I can't say for sure. All I can say is that it's worked for us."

There will be the sound of light footsteps on the end of the pier. You will both turn around. Bill's son will be there, eleven years old. "Dad, Mom says dinner's ready."

"Thanks Billy," Bill will say. You will both get up and walk to the house. Bill's son will start to take Bill's free hand but then, perhaps because you're there, think the better of it.

He will watch both of you take a swig of beer and then ask, "Dad, can I try some?"

Bill will chuckle, look at you. He will swish the bottle around and drain it until it's almost empty. Then he will hand it to his son and say, "OK — here, you can finish it. But don't tell your mom, OK? She'd be mad at both of us. . . ."

Billy will start to drain the bottle but then spit out what little he has taken into his mouth. "Eew!" he will say. "Eew! That's gross! Why do you guys drink that stuff?" he will ask.

"You'll see one day," Bill will say, "one day you'll like it too."

At dinner Karen will catch you staring at her. "What?" she will ask, good-naturedly. "What? Do I have something on my face?" She will pick up her napkin and daub at her mouth.

"'They sat down on the ground and lamented and tore their hair out, but there came no advantage to them for all their sorrowing.'" — *Odyssey* 10:567

And one time in college you arranged for a friend of yours to lose his virginity. It was at a party in your house and the friend of a friend of a girlfriend of yours, some girl you'd never met and never saw again, pointed to your roommate and asked you who he was.

"That's my roommate!" you said. "Why, you wanna meet him?"

And she said, "I dunno — maybe — maybe later."

And you said, "Wanna sleep with him?" She was cute, you were joking. And the friend of your girlfriend, some girl you knew and did see again, hit you playfully and said, "Stop it — you'll scare her off!"

But later on that same night when you were both even more drunk, she came up to you by herself when you weren't with anybody else either and said, "Yeah I do."

So you took her upstairs to the room next to yours, a single room whose occupant happened to be away for the weekend, and you told her to get undressed and get in the bed and wait and you closed the door. And you opened the door again and said, "Oh — and leave the lights off, otherwise he might get scared and wanna talk to you or something."

And then you went downstairs and found your roommate and said, "Dude, have I got a present for you." And he stumbled up the stairs after you and you told him to go into the room and leave the light off and undress and get into the bed and wait.

And the next morning you were up before both of them and you found a song you knew you had on this one album called, "Did You Do It?" and you put it on your stereo at full volume.

At the time it was hilarious. At the time you woke a lot of people up and they came into your room to complain but when you told them what was going on they thought it was funny and they all sat around your room in towels and bathrobes and boxer shorts eating cereal and donuts and watching TV and waiting for the door to the room next to yours to open.

And now, in the right crowd, you can tell this story and the story's still funny, a big hit in fact — clients love it. But it's not something you'd do now. If you did it now it wouldn't be funny.

Panthus was wrong. He should have said not, "We Trojans were," but rather, "We Trojans never were." The Romans didn't believe in Justice more than the early Greeks, they simply realized its usefulness. They realized while a man fights well for something he wants, he fights even better for something he thinks he deserves. They realized Justice could sedate the people. They realized the one god missing from the pantheon was Janus.

The Romans were the sons of Odysseus, not Achilles. Their gift to us was not civil engineering or organized warfare or even written law. Their gift to us was dissemblance.

After all, what could be more Roman than the Trojan horse?

I never dreamed about you, not once. I had dreams where you played a part, where we bought groceries or fixed a telephone. But I never dreamed about you.

"'. . . and the souls of the perished dead gathered to the place, up out of Erebos, brides, and young unmarried men, and long-suffering elders, virgins, tender and with the sorrows of young hearts upon them, and many fighting men killed in battle . . .'" — *Odyssey* 11:36

And eventually you reach a point where an old friend of yours, one outside your circle of influence, one in a different business altogether or not in business at all, maybe a writer or an artist, says, "You've changed, you never used to be this way." And you say, "I know, I know," but you don't. You think back and you decide you were always this way it's just that now you're not so afraid.

Yes, part of it is that you're just too tired to bother, you don't have the patience to worry about anyone's needs but your own. And yes, part of it is that you believe in yourself and your opinions much more because, after all, they've gotten you where you are today.

But mostly it's just that you're not so afraid. You no longer need to worry about what the majority of people think of you because now they're worried about what you think of them. Now you have so much money and thus so much power that even your parents can't help but be a little afraid of you. So now, most of the time, you can do what you want and say what you want without fear. So now, most of the time, you don't have to keep yourself hidden. Power hasn't corrupted you, it's set you free.

And you find yourself wondering if maybe that's what your old friend meant, if maybe he meant he never knew you were this way, if maybe he meant he never knew you were just trying to avoid burning any bridges all those years. You find yourself wondering if maybe it seems like you've changed to him because he never knew until now who you really were.

Ah, Nabokov, you sly old dog, you cunt, you. Even though you call Humbert a pedophile, you chose a girl just after puberty, not just before. Why would that be do you think? Could it be that you knew even your staunchest supporters would desert you if she had been younger? Could it be that you knew because she was postpubescent there would be plenty of people that would understand but that if she were prepubescent you wouldn't have found a single sympathizer? That if she were prepubescent you might as well have written a book asking its reader to pity a genocide? Could it be that all, yes all, the men you knew too, when the doors were closed, when the room was empty but for them, would look at each other and smirk and say, "Humbert was one lucky bastard, wasn't he?" Could it be that for all your respectable, scholarly exterior, you had more than one male friend who knew you well enough to say with a grin, "I can't believe you got away with that!" Could it be that you knew damn well there are plenty of people who, underneath it all, believe the saying "Old enough to bleed, old enough to breed."

Because at the end of the day, what else do we have? After the rebellions, and the struggles, and the political endeavors, after watching our backs day in and day out, guarding them not just from others but from everything, what else do we really have? A dog like the Cavaliers? A month like August? A toilet-bowl cleaner like the tragic son of Telamon? What else do we really have? What else can really make us feel alive, even if it is only for an hour or two? Is there anything else, out of all we have, that we can actually say is worth living for?

"'Achilleus, no man before has been more blessed than you, nor ever will be.'" — *Odyssey* 11:482

It is not you that we hate.

Sociopsychologists and pop culture theorists point to the annual increase in the popularity of misogynist media (e.g. the explosive success in recent years of gang bang, rough sex, and bukkake pornography) and most frequently claim this indicates that as women gain more and more power, men feel more and more threatened by that power and therefore direct more and more hatred towards women.

This is incorrect. It is not hatred we feel towards you, it is resentment. We resent you because you say you want us to treat you like men but when we treat you like men you accuse us of only treating you that way because you're women. We resent you because you say you want us to behave towards you as we would behave towards ourselves when you mean you want us to behave towards you as you behave towards yourselves. We resent you because you say you can do business the way we do business and then tell us the way we do business is "inappropriate." We resent you because you say you want things to be fair when you mean you want them to be unfair, you mean you don't want ruthless men to subjugate you as they would weaker men.

And it is the resentment that is growing. Because more and more often we hear you say, "See? We told you we were equal. We told you we could succeed in your world if the playing field was leveled," when we believe that, in fact, you succeeded in our world because we began to treat you unequally, because we unleveled the playing field.

Because it is not what is done but what is said is done that we, like you, can have problems with. After all, we are happy to use handicaps in golf or polo or video games, aren't we? Satisfied to be on a losing team as long as it beats the spread, even?

No, it is not the unfairness itself we have a problem with, it is with your saying, "We're just as strong as you, now stop punching so goddamn hard."

And it is because of this that we respect you less and less and resent you more and more. Because those are precisely the feelings we would have for men who repeated such a thing over and over and you tell us to treat you the same as men.

"So why do you put up with it?" you ask. For the same reason so many of us put up with having to ask you permission to go out with our friends, for the same reason we put up with so many of you saying you don't want us going to strip clubs anymore, for the same reason we put up with and sacrifice so many things. Because even though you may not be as strong as us, you can make us weak.

And this is why "misogynist" media is becoming more and more popular. Because the longer we keep our mouths shut, the more we want to show ourselves that, in the end, when it comes down to it, we are the ones with control over you. We desire not to suppress your developing strength but to deny our continuing compliance. We feel threatened not by your increasing power, but by our increasing weakness.

We do not hate you.

Vietnam was the only war we've ever fought where we could not expect participation or victory to bring us at least some immediate material gain.

Vietnam was the only war we've ever fought that took us into, not out of, economic hardship.

Vietnam was the only war we've ever fought simply for the sake of a cause.

How did we meet? Was it in college at some party? Did you stumble backwards into me and spill your beer on me from a plastic cup and apologize but giggle while I said it was OK, not to worry about it, even though if you'd been a man I would have picked a fight with you? Was it at our first job? Did we both start working at the same place on the same day and chance to sit next to each other when they served pasta salad and mineral water during orientation? Was it at a bar with some mutual friends? Did they mean to set us up together or did we just hit it off and surprise them all when they found out we'd been seeing each other? Was it on a deep-sea fishing boat, in a local fairground, at an automatic teller machine where you were briefly afraid I might be a mugger? Did we act shy, bold, combative because we didn't want to seem like we liked each other in case we didn't like each other? Was it cold or warm? Did the rain or the sun beat down? How did we meet?

I don't remember. But I know I thought I was lucky to have a reason to talk to you.

And what word did we choose for ourselves at the beginning of the English language? What word was chosen as the earliest colloquial term for penis?

"Cock."

From whence "cock"?

The *Oxford English Dictionary* seems to think it is derived from the compound word "stop-cock" meaning "a spout or short pipe serving as a channel for passing liquids through and having a crowning tap, the whole resembling the combed head of a cockerel."

This is the meaning from which "cock" in its modern usage is derived?

This when the word "cock" was used to denote "male" as opposed to "female" as early as 1325 A.D.?

This when the word "cock" meant "one who arouses others from slumber, a minister of religion," as early as 1386 A.D.?

This when the word "cock" meant "leader, head, chief man, ruling spirit; formerly, also, victor: said also of things," as early as 1542 A.D.?

This when the word "cock" was used colloquially after 1639 to also mean, "one who fights with pluck and spirit"?

This when as early as 1300 the word "cock" also meant "war"?

This when as early as 1386, in order to avoid blasphemy, the word "cock" was substituted for "God"?

Please.

Or maybe you were born rich, maybe you are a forest guide, a dolphin trainer. Maybe you are even happily married. It is possible you have never even thought of young girls in that way.

But then one day something happens, comes along. One day, God forbid, you have a child you don't want or one you did want is born deficient in some fashion. One day, God forbid, there is an earthquake and you were late, a day late, on the insurance payment. One day, God forbid, something happens to her, to your wife. She gets sick. She has a breakdown.

But whatever it is, you can be sure of one thing. They will turn to you and you will shoulder the weight. Without thought, without question, without looking back. Because that is what a man does. A man pays for things.

It will cost you your time. It will cost you your life. You will enter a dark, dark tunnel and even if you are, one day, blessed enough to come back into the light like Lazarus risen from the dead, you can be sure of one thing. You will not be the same.

And you cannot describe the inside of the tunnel to those who have not seen it.

And no one who has been in the tunnel ever wants to talk about it.

And suddenly a breath of fresh air once in a while will seem like something you deserve.

The decadence of the Romans was starting to believe their own sophistry and forgetting what had really built the empire.

The decadence of the Romans was allowing themselves to become enslaved to the very propaganda they had invented to set them free.

The decadence of the Romans was not beginning to value materialism too much, but too little.

You are on a plane to Guangzhou. You sent your own jet to pick someone up so you are flying first-class instead. They are building a plant for you. It will cost more than a stadium, more than a subway. When it is finished, it will be nine times larger than the block you grew up on. You know this because last Tuesday afternoon you had your personal assistant find out how big that block was, still is.

Since you boarded the plane in Los Angeles, you have been going over the numbers. You have people that have already done this for you, people whose job it is to do this and only this — accountants, investment bankers. But, unlike the racehorses you don't ride and the cars you don't wax and the paintings you're not sure you don't understand, you only have two of these. This will be your third. So for this, you are checking the numbers yourself.

When you are done, you make a call. As you suspected, all of those people have been lying to you. You are not surprised, that is the way things work. You don't even blame them, you will need to fire someone over this, someone who just leased a new car for their daughter to take to college, someone whose wife just quit her job to finally start sculpting "for real," someone with a mortgage. They were afraid. They were only protecting themselves. You would have done, will be doing, the same.

When you disconnect, the woman sitting next to you says, "Are you going to Guangzhou?"

You laugh. She looks vaguely familiar. She must be at least five eleven. She has short blond hair a little thin from too many color treatments. She wears a white, sleeveless turtleneck sweater — cashmere — and a short silk skirt. These two items cost over a thousand dollars. You know because you've bought them before. Her exposed arms and bare legs are fit, athletic, shapely but full of sinew. She must have a personal trainer, follow a rigorous exercise regimen. When she notices your eyes flicker over her legs, outstretched on the legrest, she cocks her right knee over the left, points the toe. Her calf and thigh flex under your eyes.

Since you both sat down, she has ignored you. She has been sitting next to an empty seat. It was the calculator. The laptop alone would have been fine, she would have leaned back just a little to see what you were doing, who you were. But when you produced the calculator, began to add things up for yourself, you disappeared. Then she overheard your conversation and said, "Are you going to Guangzhou?"

And you laugh because it is a direct flight.

She tells you her name, you recognize it, can place her now. She is a model, has been a model for as long as models can be models. She is not as young as she used to be. You have a friend who would call her "used up," especially if he saw her now, under the cabin's fluorescent lights. She asks you where you're staying in Guangzhou. "Oh," she says. "What a coincidence! That's where I'm staying!" It's possible it was, that she isn't going to go to the bathroom in a minute and get her agent out of bed and make him change her reservation. There are only three world-class hotels in Guangzhou, so it's possible.

She wants you to ask her what she, a world-famous model, is doing in Guangzhou, an industrial port in mainland China, so you do.

"I'm doing a spot for the World Wildlife Fund at the Zhang Bird Sanctuary," she says. This makes sense, you think, they often do things like that after thirty, when their careers are faltering, when the crevasses are too deep for the lights and the makeup to shallow out. It lets them hang on to the public eye, may even lead to some acting work.

But then, as she continues talking, you realize you are wrong. She really does love birds, can talk for hours about them. She tells you about the white-tailed eagles that live at the sanctuary. "They look like little Roman soldiers or something," she says, "stocky little soldiers with worn-out plates of brown armor all over them." She tells you how she watched a pair build their nest once, that the female — larger than the male — supervised the construction, that it made her cry. When the next round of food comes, a noodle soup, she tells you how chopsticks always remind her of the Eurasian spoonbill, this beautiful bird — as beautiful as a crane — with a spectacular crest but with a bill that looks like someone stuck a pair of chopsticks in its face. "Like this," she says, holding the chopsticks they have given you up to her mouth. With them jutting out from her face, she turns, extends her neck, holds her head up high, displays an elegant profile, and makes a sound like a duck. Her eyes come alive when she does this. In spite of yourself, you are amused. Even though this is not something she is doing just for you, is something she has done before, and in front of other men.

This part of her is actually quite charming. This part of her that she has held on to since she was a little girl. This fascination with birds that has somehow escaped destruction. How did she do that? How did she shield even that tiny piece of herself? Or was it simply chance, simply a building left standing in the rubble after an atomic blast?

Suddenly, in spite of your disinterest, you find yourself wondering if she is bisexual like so many of the models you've fucked, find yourself wondering what she would look like with your cock in her mouth. You lose the thread of what she is saying, something about land reclamation near the sanctuary, about the expansion of Guangzhou chemical plants encroaching on the reserve, about migratory patterns becoming altered, about poisoning. Something about extinction. But she finishes with a "Don't you think?" and so you are able to say, "Absolutely, I couldn't agree more," with confidence.

When you land, she pretends not to see her own car, thinks you won't notice, complains nonchalantly that her car isn't there. So you play along and invite her to share yours. Then at your hotel, if her agent hasn't managed to change her reservation yet, she makes a big fuss, is very good at pretending they've made a mistake. When she's standing at the front desk, as the bellhops take your bags upstairs, you notice that she really does still have a fantastic ass. So, wondering how many hours a day she devotes to exercising her ass alone, you tell the hotel she's a friend of yours, ask them if there isn't something they can do. She has a room within minutes. Someone else will find themselves without a room tonight.

She thanks you, of course, says, “I don’t know why they didn’t have my reservation,” tells you her room number even though she must know you heard it at the desk.

You spend all of the next day looking at the plant under construction, from very early until very late. You decide what has happened, the extra costs are Nathan’s fault. Nathan who’s worked for you for three years. Nathan who, you noticed a couple of weeks ago, just put pictures of his new son on his desk. You decide it’s Nathan who’s going to have start faxing out résumés.

When you get back to your room, you have a message. Before you retrieve it, you know who it is. And you’re right. She wants to know if you’d like to go out to the sanctuary with her tomorrow, if you’d like to see the eagles she told you about.

You are supposed to be leaving in the morning but you call your assistant and see if there’s any reason you couldn’t stay an extra day. You don’t even know why you are trying to rearrange your schedule. She’s still beautiful, certainly, still worthwhile if you didn’t have other things to do. But she’s not worth changing your plans for, is she?

Then you realize why. It’s her interest in the birds, her concern for them, the way they can still delight her as if she were five years old. That’s why you’ve decided you’ll let her try to fuck her way into your heart.

So the next day she takes you to the reserve, shows them to you, the eagles, the spoonbills, points out how even from the middle of the sanctuary you can still see the smokestacks of the refineries, how the water changes color near the protected area's boundaries. She points all of this out to you, then, after a dinner at a remarkable restaurant reserved for party officials and rich foreigners, after she bores you with the details of her flagging career, of her agent spending less and less time on her, then, after that, she fucks you anyway. She fucks you even though you are building one of the chemical refineries that is killing the only thing she loves. She fucks you anyway.

In college, you wouldn't have had the courage to ask this girl for her number. Now, the next morning, knowing you are leaving that day, she volunteers to give it to you — her cell number she points out, the most personal of her numbers. She has to ask you for yours. You give her your card, tell her that's the easiest way to get in touch with you.

But when she calls two weeks later, and again two weeks after that, you don't return her calls. You lost interest after fucking her once. That undamaged part of her was so small, it was only good for one night. Nothing more.

"'There is nothing worse for mortal men than the vagrant life, but still for the sake of the cursed stomach people endure hard sorrows. . . .'" — *Odyssey* 15:343

You're out with an old friend of yours. He started his own company a few years ago and it's been doing well. He's only thirty-five and he's worth a few hundred million, you're not sure how much. He's only thirty-five and his hair's grey. He called you up and said he wanted to go for a drink, that he needed "to vent to someone outside the industry" so he wouldn't "have a problem later."

You meet him at a bar and you catch up for a few minutes and then you ask, "So what's up?"

And he looks around suspiciously, as if in this crowded, noisy, trendy New York bar anyone would be listening. And then he moves over to your side of the booth so he can talk to you without being easily overheard and he says:

"OK. Are you ready for this one? When we first started the company we needed a little eye candy in the web development department so we pick this girl from Brazil out of the applicants. She wasn't the most qualified in terms of skill or talent — in fact she was hardly qualified at all — but she was more than qualified in the ways we wanted. We figured we could teach her what she needed to know and meanwhile we'd have something nice to look at in a department where you're usually lucky you're not turned to stone, right? And besides, what harm could she do? It was all VC money we were paying her and we could just assign her to noncritical stuff until she knew what she was doing.

"So everything's going fine. She learns the ropes, after a few months she can actually do the occasional thing we need her to do, she still looks pretty — doesn't flab out or anything — and, bonus for her, she meets this IB guy at one of our parties and ends up marrying him and — boom — green card. So she's sitting pretty and we're happy.

"Then last month we needed a new head of web development. So we bring in someone from the outside, someone who really knows what they're doing.

"And now — you ready for this? — now, out of the blue, she's fucking suing us! Not only is she stupid enough to think she's actually qualified for the job — which she isn't, not even close — but she thinks she didn't get it because she's a woman! I mean, can you appreciate the irony here? This dumb fucking cunt who only got her job, her green card, and all her fucking skills because she's a hot chick, is suing us for discrimination."

"You've got to be kidding me," you say. "That's fucking crazy — God that's such bullshit!"

"I know," says your friend. "And we're going to have to settle if we don't want the whole thing to go to court and we can't even fire her because that'll give her more leverage. It's ridiculous — she basically just said 'give me a check for fifty grand' and we have to give it to her."

"Man," you say and take a sip of your Martini.

Your friend just nods and takes a sip of his own Martini and then he says:

"You know what really gets me about this stuff? You know what really burns me? It's not the hypocrisy or the double standards like this you see every fucking day, it's not that they want us to play by one set of rules but use another set for themselves — it's the idea that life is supposed to have rules in the first place. I mean, where the fuck did anyone get the idea that life is some kind of track meet?

"Really — can you imagine the board asking me why we delayed the release of some product that was going to drive our competitors right out of the market and me saying, 'I thought they should have time to get their version ready, it wouldn't be fair otherwise'? Or what about me going to the Supreme Court and saying, 'Hey, my predecessor didn't realize how important the Asian markets were going to be so I was wondering if you could pass a law that says I get a share of those markets equal to my competitors' — it's only fair.' It would be like standing up in the middle of a war and saying, 'Listen, we ran out of ammo can you give us a day or two to get resupplied?'

"I mean, I don't know anyone who thinks life is fair, so how did so many people get the idea it's supposed to be fair? Christ, it's not like there's anybody watching, it's not like there's a goddamn referee!

"That must be why people like her think it makes sense to accuse people like me of cheating — they don't understand there's no such thing.

"They must think I think like them — not that that's not what everybody does — contrary to popular belief that's why the world's so fucked up: not because everyone sees things differently but because everyone thinks everyone sees things the same. They must think that, like them, I don't just have a goal but also some effed-up set of rules I made up for myself defining how I have to get there. Which must be why they think it makes sense to accuse people like me of racism and discrimination — they must think I give a fuck about something other than winning to believe that if I found some squad of ugly, black, femi-nazis who pumped out code better than a well-paid *Trek* convention I wouldn't hire them because they were ugly women or because they were black or both. They obviously have no clue exactly how ridiculous an accusation like that sounds, the idea I'd turn down some competitive advantage because of some fucking belief of mine — it's crazy!"

And he looks at you and you look at him and you realize he's not talking anymore and you say, "Sorry, say that again — I thought those girls were getting pissed off at us but they aren't, they're checking us out."

And he says, "Really? Which girls?" and turns around.

Because in ancient Athens, to get to Plato's academy you had to walk through the public cemetery for those killed in war.

Because the Peloponnesian War began in 431 B.C., *The Trojan Women* was written in 415 B.C., *Lysistrata* was written in 411 B.C., and Athens lost the Peloponnesian War in 404 B.C.

Because the great vanity is not thinking we can win, it's thinking we don't need to fight.

And there was that time when I had the flu but was supposed to give an important pitch the next day. That time you stayed up with me almost all night. You couldn't help with the work but you made me tea and toast and soup and made sure I was warm enough.

And the next day when I left, uncertain if what I'd done was enough, uncertain that I could pull things off because I was sick, you really did say, "Don't worry, everything will be fine." And you really did kiss me.

"I love you," I said. And, right there, right then, I did.

"'. . . there is no suppressing the ravenous belly, a cursed thing, which bestows many evils on men, seeing that even for its sake the strong-built ships are handled across the barren great sea, bringing misfortune to enemies.'" — *Odyssey* 17:286

You are watching TV on a Sunday afternoon. Flipping through the channels you stop briefly on a women's talk show. The hosts are women, the audience is women, they are discussing women's issues.

It takes you a minute to figure out what they are actually discussing but it seems like some famous supermodel in her twenties just married some man in his eighties worth a few hundred million. The hosts and their guests and the audience are all taking turns saying how disgusting it is. And then one of the women in the audience gets called on and stands up and says, "I'll tell you one thing — if I was going to marry an eighty-four-year-old man, he'd have to be worth a lot more than three hundred and forty million dollars!"

And she brings down the house. The hosts, the guests, the audience all cheer and clap and laugh. And it's a big joke. Except you know it isn't, you know the reason they're all laughing is that their idea of integrity is not whether or not they're for sale, but rather how much they think they're worth.

And so believe me when I tell you peace is a Gulfstream V or a one-off dress by Coco Chanel. Believe me when I tell you guilt is a Loire Valley château. Believe me when I tell you they are both just one more luxury.

You are in a department store buying some cologne and you look up and across the counter, on the other side, on the women's side, are two high school girls and they are staring at you and when you catch them they look caught and one of them says "oh shit," and they duck behind a sign, giggling.

And it occurs to you that things are also so much easier with them, with those girls that, as misguided as they may be, are not yet afraid, those girls young enough to still show interest in you by doing more than simply not resisting when you show interest in them. With them it's so simple to get to the bottom line. With all the other things you need patience for, with all the other things you have to work on, who wants to put time and energy into wooing, into something that's supposed to be a pleasure?

"Now as these two were conversing thus with each other, a dog who was lying there raised his head and ears. This was Argos, patient-hearted Odysseus' dog, whom he himself raised, but got no joy of him, since before that he went to sacred Ilion. In the days before, the young men had taken him out to follow goats of the wild, and deer, and rabbits; but now he had been put aside, with his master absent, and lay on a deep pile of dung . . . covered with dog ticks. Now, as he perceived that Odysseus had come close to him, he wagged his tail, and laid both his ears back; only he now no longer had the strength to move any closer to his master, who, watching him from a distance, without Eumaios noticing, secretly wiped a tear away. . . .

"Then, O swineherd Eumaios, you said to him . . . : 'This, it is too true, is the dog of a man who perished far away. If he were such, in build and performance, as when Odysseus left him behind, when he went to Ilion, soon you could see his speed and his strength for yourself. Never could any wild animal, in the profound depths of the forest, escape, once he pursued. He was very clever at tracking. But now he is in bad times. . . . the women are careless, and do not look after him; and serving men, when their masters are no longer about, to make them work, are no longer willing to do their rightful duties. For Zeus of the wide brows takes away one half of the virtue from a man, once the day of slavery closes upon him.'

"So he spoke, and went into the strongly-settled palace, and strode straight on, to the great hall and the haughty suitors. But the doom of dark death now closed over the dog, Argos, when, after nineteen years had gone by, he had seen Odysseus." — *Odyssey* 17:290

Maybe there is a priest. Maybe every now and then you walk up the broad stone steps of a cathedral and through that smaller door in the bigger door. Maybe you go when it is empty so nothing but the pews stretch away from you towards the altar, dim in the distance. Maybe there is a coughing coming from somewhere but you never see the person who coughs, are never even sure if you're looking for them in the right direction because of the resonance and the echoes.

Or maybe it is not a cathedral. Maybe you pass through the gate of a temple compound into a dusty courtyard with a black gong shaped like a bell. And you walk to the small building off to the side where devoted laywomen, older, fatter, take donations for roof tiles.

Or maybe you make an appointment and visit a synagogue, finding your way into the back, into the rabbi's study paneled with dark wood and with only one small window in front of which sits a sickly ivy.

Maybe, if you are religious after a fashion, you feel guilty all the time. Not just for the sexual exploits, almost every single one of which has been "sinful" by some definition, but also for everything else. You feel guilty about doing business the way you do business. Even though some part of you believes you should be praised for it, even rewarded for it, you feel guilty about winning.

So you go to confessional, you pay for prayers in your name to be painted on roof tiles, you ask for advice from a man who has never competed. And you are absolved or prayed for or given advice, it doesn't matter what. Because it won't help. It can never help.

And eventually you will stop going through that smaller door in the bigger door, stop passing through the temple gate, stop making appointments. Or you will stop winning. Because there can be no religions for winners. Because even if God really does clothe the lilies in the field, he won't provide you with a present for your wife's birthday. Even if Buddha really does grant enlightenment to those who have forsaken worldly ways, that would mean you'd have to send your son to public school and you'll be damned if he has to attend the one in your district.

But ah, Nabokov, why did Quilty have to pay? It wasn't a movie of the week, you didn't have to worry about the advertisers pulling out ("pulling out"?). And you must have known the Quiltys of the world never pay. So why did you do that, you coward, you pussy, you?

You have no idea how it happened. You know you were staying with Jonathan, at his villa on the cliff in St. Barths. You know that it began the day he and Marjorie and Tamsin went out to shop for batik leaving you alone with Cassandra. But you were as surprised as everyone else that it happened.

You were lying by the pool and she came out for a swim. She had been there a month already, her skin was already tan. And you could see so much of it even when you just glanced up from your book, a masturbatory, soapbox piece by a CEO you knew very well.

And then when she came up out of the pool after doing some laps, she didn't dry herself off. You think that was what did it, that was what broke your will to resist. Those beads of water on her smooth brown skin, those beads of water caught up in the transparent down that seemed to cover most of her body, those beads of water that smelled like suntan oil. She came up to your deck chair and knelt down near your head. You pretended not to notice her. She leaned over your book, her long, wet, black hair hanging down one side of her face, the side away from you, and just barely caressing the rough-cut edges of the hardcover's paper. You could see the water seeping into the paper, ruining the book. But you didn't move for fear of frightening her away, as if she were a wild animal, for fear of no longer being able to smell her so close. That smell of chlorine and suntan oil and sun and something else, something clean, something really only young girls smell like.

"Whatcha reading?" she asked.

And while you told her she just stared at you, nodding as if she were listening but her enormous green eyes wandering all over your face, her eyes wandering as if she had managed to get very close to some deep-sea creature and was only going to have this one chance to study it. She had the most beautiful lips, so full, so turgid. And her nose was so tiny, smaller than your thumb.

Or maybe it wasn't the drops of water. Maybe it was the bee. Maybe if the bee hadn't landed on your chest, hadn't kind of somehow gotten caught and confused and angry in the seam of the book, maybe if that hadn't happened then nothing else would.

But it did happen. It did land there, just as you finished explaining and she had yelped, leapt back, and you had slammed the book shut but somehow missed the bee and it had stung your chest, right at the base of the sternum. And then it was your turn to yelp and leap up and the dead bee tumbled down your body and onto your towel.

She had come closer cautiously, come closer as you swore and watched the welt grow on your chest. She had looked down at the bee and then pushed at it reservedly with her middle finger.

"They die once they sting," you managed to say, not wanting to seem like it hurt too much, which it did, it stung like a motherfucker.

"I know that," she said looking at you and rolling her eyes, "I've just never actually seen one die." "Oh my gosh, look at your chest," she added.

And you looked down, trying very hard not to spend too long on her recently risen breasts still glistening with dew, on her still-forming hips, on her new waist, on her brown belly with its belly button like a puncture, on the bony mound that pushed out between her legs, you looked down and saw the welt had grown considerably in just a few seconds.

As you went inside, as she took your hand to lead you inside to get you some aloe vera, you noticed the wet shades her knees and the balls of her feet had left on the sunbaked flagstone, left on the sunbaked flagstone where she had been kneeling when she had just gotten out of the pool. Like the Shroud of Turin, you thought.

She took you into the kitchen, made you sit down, and padded off to some bathroom or other. The kitchen smelled like her, like all those smells she smelled like.

When she came back you went to get up, to reach out to take it from her, and she pushed you back down, said, "Sit down." And you obeyed her, because it was really your obedience that made you sit down, not her push. She couldn't have pushed you over even if she had used all her weight and strength, couldn't have even moved you.

She squirted some aloe vera on her palm, squirted another clean, fresh scent into the air to mingle with the others, and scooped a little bit up with the fingers of her other hand and rubbed it into the wound.

Then, without looking at you, she kissed it. She opened her mouth slightly and kissed it.

When you didn't push her away in horror, she kissed it some more, gently, her lips puckered but closed. At last she looked up at you. She didn't need to say anything. You had to have your mouth on hers. You crushed your mouth to hers so hard it hurt you both a little. Her tongue was so small yet so strong, so resilient. You had her up on the counter in a second, had her legs spread and hooked around you, her bikini top yanked down exposing her little breasts to your hungry mouth, her bikini bottoms pulled aside, your fingers inside her as your other hand pulled her body to you by the small of her back. She couldn't have weighed more than a hundred and five pounds. Her hands just pushed up on the underside of the cabinets, kept her from slipping too far back, kept her from banging her head against them. You pulled your trunks down and entered her. Because of her tanlines, it was over very quickly. You couldn't contain yourself inside her. But it was the best orgasm you'd had in years. She opened her eyes at last, had been keeping them closed since you hoisted her up on the counter.

"Oh God, what have I done," was the first thing you thought. And it must have shown on your face because the first thing she said, as she pulled off you, as she straightened her top and bottoms, as she slipped off the counter and got some paper towels, the first thing she said was, "Don't worry I'm on the Pill." And then as she wiped up the counter she added, "And I wasn't a virgin or anything either, if that's what you're worried about." She said it as if "virgin" were comparable to "neo-Nazi." But that wasn't what you were worried about. That wasn't it at all. You're not even sure you were worried. As she threw the towels away, she said with a grin, "You may want to think about pulling your trunks up, I think I heard a car."

Or maybe it wasn't the bee. Maybe it would have happened without the drops of water or the bee. Maybe it would have happened differently, but it would have happened.

By the time Tamsin came in, you were back out by the pool, pretending to read, your heart still pounding. She was wearing a one-piece bathing suit and a new batik gown open on top of it.

"What happened to your chest?" she said, concerned. She wore sunglasses. You couldn't see her eyes.

And then that night the "girls," as they called themselves, cooked. And they enlisted Cassandra to chop the vegetables. "She hasn't really learned to do anything worthwhile in the kitchen yet," you heard Marjorie sigh to Tamsin. Still in her bikini, still barefoot, a kind of woven, multicolored bracelet around one ankle, a bracelet you knew the feel of pressing into your gripping palm, Cassandra insisted on using the spot on the counter where you'd fucked her to do the job they gave her.

But when she sat down to dinner like that, her mother made her go upstairs to change. You stared at your plate and speared the vegetables she'd cut and tried not to think about her getting changed in her room, about her naked body, about the triangular patches of pale skin you now knew she had around her nipples and her pussy. But you still got an erection.

And then that night, with the lights off, you couldn't sleep. So you cupped Tamsin's breasts in your hands and she said "oooo — hello . . ." and rolled over and stroked underneath your cock with her fingers, stroked your cock precisely the way you liked best, and then climbed on top of you and fucked you pretty hard. If you kept your hands off her, if you just lay back and let her ride you there in the dark, you could pretend it was Cassandra. You could pretend it was your friend's daughter, that is, except for the smell. When you came it was because you were thinking about Cassandra's mouth, open slightly, moaning almost imperceptibly as you fucked her.

When you woke up the next day, you were in a panic. For some reason, you were terrified she had told her mother, confessed in sobs, made it seem like you had seduced her or worse. You brushed your teeth and you looked in the mirror and you rehearsed in your mind saying things like, "That's ridiculous!" But you knew you could never be convincing. You knew they'd see the guilt on your face. When you went down to breakfast, you felt like you thought you would if you were going to your own execution. You couldn't look at Tamsin. What would she say? Would she scream at you or, unable to bear it (what? the shame? the anger?), would she quietly walk out of the room? She asked you what was wrong on the way down the stairs. "Nothing," you said. "Nothing's wrong."

But at the breakfast table, everything had been normal. And as you went outside to read, as you breathed a sigh of relief, you swore you'd stay away from her for the remainder of the month. Later Tamsin had said, "You're in a good mood!" and you'd replied, "Sure — why not?"

But a couple of days later, during which Cassandra had spoken to you no more than necessary, you and Jonathan were reading out by the pool and she came out and asked her father if he would take her shopping. He said he didn't want to, that he'd take her the next day. She had her back to you and was wearing faded jeans that could have been painted on. When he said that, in her disappointment she shifted her weight from one foot to the other and her ass moved those jeans up and down as she did so and you found yourself saying, "I'll take her, Jonathan."

And she turned around and looked at you and you could see she wasn't wearing a bra under her loose tank top.

"Oh that's really nice of you but don't worry about it, it's not necessary," Jonathan said.

"No, really," you insisted, prompted by the way the tank top hung from her nipples in the breeze, "it's fine, I'm not getting anything done here anyway."

"Well, if you insist," he said. "That's really nice of you, Geoff — thank Geoff, sweetie, he's doing you a favor!"

She squinted at you, the sun was behind you. "Thanks Mr. Martinson," she said. She had called you Geoff for years but had been calling you Mr. Martinson for the last few days, had been making a point of using your name all the time.

You took the Jeep and she made you drive down a deserted track to a cliff overlooking the ocean. You fucked her from behind in the back of the Jeep, she didn't even bother taking her jeans off all the way. You managed to control yourself longer this time but it was probably because you were nervous. You kept looking back up the dirt road to see if anyone was coming. She barely moved, stared out at the ocean the entire time. But she did look over her shoulder at you and smile when you came. You fucked her twice more that afternoon.

As you drove back down the track, another car drove past, heading for the cliff. You couldn't see who was inside but she said, "That would have been funny, wouldn't it?!" You didn't answer her.

When you got home her father asked if she'd gotten anything and when she said, "No. I couldn't find anything I liked," he joked with you, "Huh — maybe you should take her shopping more often — when she goes with me she always manages to spend a fortune!"

But again when you woke the next morning, you felt fear. No, not fear this time, worry. You were worried. You brushed your teeth without practicing a word. You managed to walk into breakfast with your head up. Cassandra and Marjorie were already there. "Morning, Geoff!" said Marjorie pleasantly. You smiled back, "Morning, Marjorie." And it even gave you the audacity to add, "Morning, Cassandra."

"Good morning Mr. Martinson," she said, returning your smile.

And from then on you weren't even worried, from then on it went on untroubled. You had to invent excuses to be alone with her as much as possible, certainly. You caught a cold, faked a sprained ankle, had so many allergies that after a couple of weeks Tamsin said, "You poor dear, this just isn't your summer is it?" You said things like, "No go on, don't worry about me, I have all those books I want to get through," more times than you can remember. But it was worth it to get beyond the frantic, panting gropings in the hallways. It was worth it to get what you wanted.

Not that there weren't close calls.

One day, quite early on, you were lying by the pool with everyone. Cassandra was sunning herself on an inflatable sunbed in the pool and you were wearing your darkest sunglasses so you could pretend to read while you looked over the top of the book at her drifting around there. You were so clever you even remembered to turn the pages regularly. And then suddenly Tamsin, lying next to you on another chair, said very quietly, "Umm, Geoff, Ah-hem!" And your heart nearly exploded out of your chest but you used every ounce of self-control you had to look at her calmly and say, "What?" as innocently as you possibly could. And she frowned and glanced around and jabbed a finger with staccato movements towards your waist. Your heart began to slow. "What?" you said again, the ignorance genuine this time, you said as you lifted your book above your head to look under it. You had an erection. Embarrassed, you shifted around until it was hidden. Tamsin said, "Maybe I should be worried." Again, your heart picked up, "What? Why?" you asked. "Because it looks like interest rates turn you on more than I do." And when you stared at her blankly, wondering what the hell she was talking about, wondering what answer you could give that wouldn't give you away without you even knowing it, when you stared at her like that she rolled her eyes and pointed at your book. You looked at the page you were on. It was about interest rates. You didn't even know which book you had been pretending to read.

And there was the time it was rainy so everyone was inside and you went into the media room, a big open space with lots of entrances, and Cassandra was in there alone stretched out on the couch watching some Disney cartoon. She was just wearing an oversize T-shirt, her bare legs with their recently acquired curves curled up beside her like bows cut from green wood. You couldn't help yourself. From experience you knew she wore nothing beneath that T-shirt except her panties and you had to sit down next to her and slide your hand up the smooth brown skin of her thigh and slip it under her shirt and pull her panties aside and gently stroke that slit between her legs and go to kiss her. But she smacked your hand and pulled her head away in irritation. "Stop it," she said, "I'm trying to watch this." So you pulled your hand away and it was a good thing too because right at that moment Marjorie came into the room. And the two of you must have looked guilty because when she saw you she said in a mock scold, "What have you two been up to? It's thick as thieves in here!" But before you could answer, she went on talking but just to Cassandra this time and said, "Have you been telling Geoff all your secrets again?" And she came up close behind her daughter, stood behind the couch where you both sat, and gently pulled her daughter's hair back into a ponytail and caressed it and carefully pulled her daughter's head back so they were looking at each other upside down. And then she said, without looking at you, still stroking her daughter's hair, still looking at her daughter, "She really trusts you, you know, Geoff — she told me so . . . my little angel." And she kissed Cassandra on her forehead and let her return her head upright, facing you. Then, with her mother behind her and no one behind you, Cassandra blew you a little kiss. Then she shifted her body just slightly so you could see up her T-shirt, shifted her body just slightly so you could see her panties were still pulled to one side. You glanced at Marjorie who was now absorbed in the cartoon, trying to figure out what was going on, one hand still resting absentmindedly on the back of her daughter's head. You suddenly felt like you were going to throw up. You suddenly wondered what the hell you thought you were doing.

And there was the time shortly before you left when you were all arguing at dinner and you went upstairs to get a book that proved your point and when you turned around to leave the room Cassandra was in the doorway. That time there were several guests, people you both knew who were on the island that weekend and everyone had dressed for dinner. That time she wore makeup and earrings and a man's white shirt and a miniskirt despite her mother's objections. That time you paused and stood still with the book already in your hands and when you paused she knew you wouldn't resist at all so she walked into the room, still not confident on the carpet in her heels she walked into the room and pushed you back onto the bed and knelt between your legs and unzipped your pants and pulled your already erect cock out with one hand while she unbuttoned her shirt with the other. Then you leaned up off the bed, supported yourself on your elbows, and watched while she rubbed the head of your cock over her nipples, watched as she slipped all she could of it into her tiny mouth — barely more than the head, watched as, just as you came, she pulled her mouth off you and held your cock close to her cheek, watched as, with a smile, with her eyes closed and her head thrown back, with both hands, she rubbed your semen into her face, her throat, her breasts. It was only then you noticed she'd left the door open, only then you noticed that, you who was always so careful about everything. And, noticing, you suddenly panicked, shoved yourself back in your pants, pulled her to her feet by her arms, her enormous green eyes opening at your touch, and pushed her into your bathroom to clean herself up. That time you made her go downstairs first, that time you had to change your pants, that time you came back downstairs after fifteen minutes, relieved to see Cassandra already there and chatting pleasantly with the old woman next to her, when you came downstairs and said, waving the book in the air, "Sorry! Couldn't find it." That time when, after you sat down, you noticed Tamsin studying you with a frown. That time your wife leaned over and said quietly in your ear while you looked around at everyone else, everyone else absorbed in other conversations, while you played with your wineglass, that time she whispered, "Why did you change your pants?" That time you had no answer.

But these were exceptions. For the most part the two of you had nothing to fear. When the house was empty you fucked her everywhere. You fucked her out by the pool, in the shower, on the living room couch. She told you to choke her, panted, "No — no — keep doing it," when you apologized for banging her head against the headboard, asked you shyly if you'd call her your "little teen bitch." Even wanted you to fuck her in the ass but decided it was too painful after you eagerly agreed.

And yet the night you would — wish you could — repeat again and again without hesitation, the night you have absolutely no regrets about even now Tamsin has found out and left and Jonathan and Marjorie are trying to prosecute you, a case you're told they don't have a hope of winning, the night you remember the most vividly, that night had nothing to do with sex.

It was the night the four of you were supposed to have left Cassandra alone and flown over to Paradise Island for dinner and gambling and stayed in a hotel but instead you pretended you had sprained your ankle. You had been thinking about it for days. As soon as you had all agreed on the excursion, you the most enthusiastically, you had begun machinating over the best way to be left behind with Cassandra, all alone with her for an entire night. A whole night! It was the first thing in your life you found you didn't just want, didn't simply desire, you who'd desired so much and gotten it all, it was, instead, something you had to have, something you felt you couldn't live without, would go mad without. You knew you would do anything for it, pay anything for it, degrade yourself in whatever way necessary for it. If you'd thought it might help, you would have possibly killed for it. Yet, in the end, all you had to do was fake a sprained ankle.

And so you had her to yourself for an entire night. And as soon as it had started, as soon as Tamsin and Jonathan and Marjorie got in that beat-up island cab to head for the tiny island airport ("Look after Geoff, dear, make sure he has everything he needs!"), as soon as you couldn't believe this was really going to happen, as soon as you couldn't believe you were actually going to be this lucky, this blessed, as soon as that, you knew this night was going to be unequaled by any other night of your life.

But not because of the sex. Not that you didn't have sex, of course, and more times in one night than in a very long time (at least for you). But because afterwards, when it got late, when she fell asleep, you just lay there holding her young body against yours, as close to yours as possible. Smelling her. Staring into the dark. You just lay there like that all night. Awake. Not moving. You didn't sleep at all, you who was always so tired. You didn't want to waste one moment you could possibly be enjoying that sensation, that sensation you were fairly certain you'd never felt and doubted you'd have the chance to feel again. That sensation of being alive.

And in the morning when she woke, she kissed you, played wife, made you breakfast, said, "You look tired." "Must be the ankle," you joked. She laughed then and also later when you said the same thing to Tamsin when she said the same thing to you. Although you had said it quite differently that second time.

And yet even after that, closer to when you were supposed to be leaving, she still began to get cute. She left a copy of *Lolita* in Tamsin's bathroom. She flashed you her tits after you and her father walked past her in a hallway. She even somehow snuck through your room at night and left a message on your bathroom mirror in lipstick — "Couldn't sleep," it said, "kept thinking about your cock."

And so the first time you were alone, the first chance you got, you grabbed her by both arms and shook her and shouted, "What the hell do you think you're doing?! Do you think this is some kind of game!?" And she had started to cry. And you had let her go right away, apologized. And snuffling, holding back tears, she said, "I thought you'd think it was funny!" Then she wiped her nose on the back of her hand and ran upstairs. You barely had time to comfort her and get her looking decent before the others came home.

At breakfast the next morning you nearly choked on your coffee when Jonathan told her to come here and looked closely at her arms and asked her where she got the bruises barely visible on her tan skin just above her biceps. But she was very good at lying. She gave nothing away. She just shrugged and said she didn't know, in the pool maybe. Even though you could make out a mark your ring had left, Jonathan believed her. "Well, just be more careful OK? I love you — I wouldn't want anything to happen to you," and he kissed her on the forehead and she nodded and said she loved him too and sat back down. Then Jonathan looked at you and rolled his eyes and said, "Kids!" You snorted in agreement, conspiratorially, and drank some more coffee.

But when you did leave at last, she confused you. When you did leave at last, to your amazement, she had been crying. When you did leave at last, she stopped you alone in the hallway and said, "But I love you."

Then she collapsed against you, sobbing, hugging you. And you patted her on the back while you looked up and down the corridor in case someone came. You didn't understand. You didn't think it had anything to do with that. You didn't think it had anything to do with that at all.

It is possible to determine how important a thing is to a society by the number of words that society has for it. The number of subtle distinctions shows how much time they have spent thinking about it, how familiar they are with it, how important a part it plays in their lives. Thus, the Eskimo have twenty-two words for snow; the Bedouin, thirty-one words for sand.

From these kinds of examples the argument is also derived that to understand a culture, one must first understand its language.

And it is also these kinds of examples that make some cognitive scientists and linguists believe that language is the most useful tool we have for understanding the brain's higher functions. The brain receives information about the world through the senses and then organizes that information. And because language is entirely an abstract creation of the brain designed to help convey that organization, the idea is that if we can understand how language is designed, we can then understand how the brain functions by a kind of reverse engineering. The idea is that words expose us.

And some of the exhaustion, a good part perhaps, you can't say how much exactly, some of the exhaustion is purely physical.

You always seem to be moving. You always seem to be in planes or cars, always going from one place to another where you sit and talk for an hour or two and then move on. You spend months at a time away from any of your houses. You're always taking vitamins, herbal supplements, always terrified you're going to get sick, terrified you're not going to be able to make a meeting, appear before a major shareholder.

So the last thing you want to do when you do reach somewhere you can call your own, when you do have a second to just sit still and do nothing, the last thing you want to do is anything.

And maybe this is why, when you're visiting a line and the manager who's showing you around says to one of the workers over the noise of the machines, "Vikki, you're still here? Lot of overtime today, huh?" and she really does wipe the sweat off her face and say, "WHAT?" and he says, "LOT OF OVERTIME TODAY," and she smiles and nods and looks at you and shrugs and says, "MORTGAGE WON'T PAY ITSELF, RIGHT?" this is why then you can say, "I HEAR THAT!"

Except you do and you don't. Not because even though you work just as hard you're hardly worried about making ends meet, but because she can go home and take a bath and wash it all away. Because, even if only for a little while, she can forget it all. Because she, unlike you, does not live in perpetual terror of losing. And she never will.

You are helping your daughter with a school project she is doing on cruelty to animals, on the various ways in which animals are exploited by humans, and you come across an interview with a man who commanded a K-9 unit in Vietnam. When asked if he thought using dogs in war was cruel, if he felt sorry for them because they didn't ask to be there, because they had no control over whether they were there or not, he answered, "Let me tell you something about these dogs — they fucking love it, they love being part of a team, they love having a purpose, they love to work. When we're just sitting around waiting for an op, they get bored. Even when they're being petted and fed scraps and played with, they'll sit around and whine and groan and huff and puff until we get orders. And then they're the first ones in the truck. They leap up there and pant and grin and pace until the truck starts moving. While we're sitting there wondering if we'll make it back, they can't wait to get there. And I know what you're going to say, 'They don't understand they might die out there — they don't know about pain.' Well let me tell you something else — even if they get wounded they don't want to stop going.

"If you actually knew these dogs, if you'd spent time with them instead of thinking they're like your little poodle at home, you'd know that you don't feel the most sorry for them when they get hurt. You feel the most sorry for them when the next op comes around and they run over to the truck on three legs or misjudge the jump into the back because they're missing an eye. You feel the most sorry for them when the truck drives off and you look back and see them standing there panting, wondering why they're not allowed to come, wondering what they did wrong. You feel the most sorry for them when you see that they don't know their life is over, not when they don't understand it might end."

And yet sometimes, times when you are in the best of moods, when everything has just come together the way you'd planned, when you haven't begun to worry about the next step, a girl will walk past with her friends. She will be wearing a skirt you would never let your daughter wear and her legs will be longer than her torso and you will turn and watch her until she disappears and it will be then and only then that you will realize you haven't been breathing.

"'There I found Odysseus standing among the dead men he had killed, and they covered the hardened earth, lying piled

on each other around him. You would have been cheered to see him, spattered over with gore and battle filth, like a lion.'"
— Eurykleia to Penelope, *Odyssey* 23:45

You are taking your daughter out to dinner. She is your oldest, from your first marriage. Her name is Jennifer or Sandy or something reasonable like that, nothing too unusual, your first wife was never one to take risks.

She is a freshman at one of the most progressive colleges in the country and you are at one of the restaurants near campus that many of the students go to for dates and other special occasions. They seat you next to a young couple in the middle of their meal, from their conversation about what movies they like, obviously on a first date. After you sit down your daughter leans across the table a little bit and gestures for you to come close and when you do she says in a loud whisper, "That girl's my floor's dorm adviser — she's a women's studies major — she is such a pain in the ass!"

"Do you want to move?" you whisper back.

"No," she says in a normal voice as she leans back. "This is cool."

And you have a perfectly pleasant meal. You were very lucky, your daughter has never held it against you that you left her mother for a younger woman nor that you left that younger woman for a girl only slightly older than her. She's very progressive, your daughter, very forgiving, very understanding. She knows everything, wonders why people can't just compromise and get along. And this matters to you, it really does. You think it would make you unhappy if she was angry with you.

But she isn't, the two of you get along extraordinarily well, in fact. Sometimes, in fact, when you see your friends with their children, you wonder if the reason you relate so much better to your daughter than they do to theirs is precisely because you spend so much time with a girl almost as young as she is, because you can walk into her dorm room and see a poster on her wall and say, "Cindy and I checked out their show last month" instead of, "They're a band, are they?"

And in the middle of your meal, after they clear away the oysters, after she says, "Yes, I would like another glass," as Jennifer or Sandy or Catherine or whatever her name is starts telling you about one of her professors, how much she likes him, how he's taken an interest in her, as she starts doing that you notice that the waitress just brought the check to the couple next to you.

And although the girl doesn't even reach for it, the boy snatches it up. "How much is it?" she asks, reaching down to get her purse from the floor next to her.

"Don't worry about it," he says. "Let me get it."

And she says, "Are you sure?" still leaning over to one side.

And he says, "Absolutely."

And she says, "Well, okayyy . . . if you're sure . . ." sitting up straight at last.

And he smiles at her and proudly counts out some tiny sum, less than the cost of the bottle of wine you and your daughter are drinking. Because of where he is sitting, across from her, you know he couldn't have seen what you saw sitting next to them. You know he couldn't have seen that when she reached down for her purse, she never, at any point, actually reached down far enough to touch it.

And you wonder what the hell she's thinking. If he was some new friend of hers, she never would have let him pay. Or if she did, she would know that at some point, if she wanted to remain friends, she'd have to pay him back later with money not "friendship," that later she'd have to cover the cost of the drinks or the movie. She'd know enough not to mix money and friendship, know enough not to let the balance of accounts between her and a friend become imbalance, so why with a potential boyfriend does she think it's OK not only to let him pay, but to start off their entire relationship that way? Even if she believes he is only paying for the pleasure of her company, even if, in fact, he is, would she expect a friend to buy that from her? Does she think in this case it's "romantic"? Does it make her feel "special," like a "princess"?

What happens later? What happens if this relationship works out for a while, for long enough for them to get married, to have children, what happens later when she is too old or too damaged or both to give him the things he was paying for all those years? What happens then? Doesn't she realize the cost of his worrying about money, about bearing weight, about being protector and provider, the cost of his covering the mud with his cloak, the cost of his "doing the right thing" if she gets pregnant, the cost of his holding open doors will be far more than her half of all the meals they will ever share together? Doesn't she realize that later, the cost of his chivalry will be his feeling he has earned the right to be dishonest every now and then?

And yet, as they stand up, she knows enough to hand him the doggie bag full of the food she only half ate and say, "Here, you should take this."

And you turn to your daughter and interrupt her in the middle of a sentence you haven't been listening to anyway and say, "Annie, promise me something — don't ever let a man pay for you. Ever."

And she looks at you and frowns and then raises the frown high on her forehead and glances off to the side for a second and says, "Okayyy, Dad . . ."

"I mean it," you say, "really."

And she says, "I promise, I promise . . . geez!" then, "Hey, can we try and get some more oysters before the other food comes?"

But we do love our plumbing and our penicillin, don't we?

And yet, at the end of the day, wouldn't you feel a little bit silly if you said what we all think whether we know we think it or not? If you said, "Well, yes, actually I do feel like I should be treated like a conquering hero for closing that deal with

Packard. I do feel like I deserve gifts of women and gold and respect." Wouldn't this seem a little bit silly? After all, it's not like you killed anyone.

Odysseus was a hero to the Greeks but a villain to the Trojans. And when is it not such?

But you'd never complain. Those men that bitch really bother you, those men who say, "Man, I can't believe I have to do another trade show," and "Damn it, I don't want to work another weekend." It's not like they couldn't quit anytime if they really wanted to.

And there are so many other possibilities. There is the local waitress that, to his surprise, takes an interest in the utility worker on his hunting trip up into the mountains, perhaps because, for her, it is simply enough to overhear him mention he lives near something she's always wanted to see. There is the college student approaching the guest speaker after his talk and asking him so many questions, displaying such interest, that he finds himself asking her if she'd like to talk about it over dinner. There is the teacher and student bumping into each other outside of school, over a weekend, going for coffee together. There is the teacher and student alone in the classroom after most people have left the building. There really are starlets and directors, confessors and priests, actresses and politicians. There really are interns, baby-sitters.

The money just presents more opportunities, more temptations, creates interest more often. Just because the money is a facilitator doesn't mean it can't happen without it.

But it does mean the man who tells his wife he was working late feels less guilty than the man who says he was working overtime.

Everyone forgets that Odysseus and Achilles and Agamemnon, all of them, all the Argives and the Trojans both, all of them were real people.

Or perhaps when your heart begins to beat fast in the conference room, you don't speak up or you back down. Perhaps you don't want to make waves, enemies, a fool of yourself. Perhaps you have an idea you're pretty sure is great but not absolutely sure and as much as you'd really like to quit your job and start your own company, you worry about making enough to live off, about backup plans, about how much is in the savings account that never has enough.

Maybe when you go to get another bottle of red from the kitchen, when your best friend's daughter or your daughter's best friend corners you, when she surprises the hell out of you by pressing her body up against yours as you turn around with the bottleneck in one hand and the corkscrew in the other, maybe when that happens, you ask her what she's doing. Maybe when that happens, you do the "right" thing and she apologizes, gets incredibly embarrassed, calls you "Mr." whatever, says she's never had this much wine before, hurries back into the living room grabbing a box of crackers on the way. Maybe when that happens, you start to follow her but then decide you'd better open the bottle of wine in the kitchen so, before you rejoin the party, your erection has time to go down.

And maybe, just maybe, as you open the wine, as you slip with the knife when trying to cut the foil away and nick your thumb, your best friend or daughter comes into the kitchen and asks if you've seen their daughter or best friend. And you say, "She was just here — I thought she went back in the other room." And they say, "Oh — that's strange — must have just missed her," and they turn around and leave and you think to yourself, "See?"

And then you'll lie there that night when she's asleep (wife) and think how you could never do it, how by doing it you could lose everything you have — the house, the wife you're not sure you don't love — how your daughter probably wouldn't speak to you again or not for a long time at least. It's not much, it's true, but it's more than most have, it's better than jail where you'd get anally raped, it's better than working at McDonald's.

And eventually you'll tell yourself you really did do the right thing.

But then you'll find you won't be able to sleep. Then you'll find every time you close your eyes you don't remember how she smelled, you can actually smell how she smelled. Then you'll find every time you look at the clock it's gotten later and later and that soon you won't be able to get the bare minimum amount of sleep you know you need to function at work so you'll get up and go into the bathroom and lock the door and jerk off over how her T-shirt clung to her nipples like a plastic film for covering food, over how hard her nipples felt up against you, like two little buttons up against you, over how somewhere in there the wine got opened and you poured it over her naked thighs and over her lower belly and over her pussy — which you're somehow sure must be tight and thinly furred and a very pale pink indeed — and you licked it up, her muscles flexing taut with every flick of your tongue, her pelvis bucking into your face, bruising your nose. Then you'll find it doesn't take you very long to cum.

But as you walk back to the bedroom, you'll suddenly start worrying that maybe because you rejected her she'll make something up, she'll say something happened when it didn't. A friend of yours told you about a friend of his, a high school teacher in Florida, who got fired just because a girl said he'd been coming on to her when it really was the other way around.

So then you'll lay awake wondering if that could happen to you, trying to remember everything you've seen her do, everything you've heard her say, trying to figure out what sort of person she is, if that's something she'd do, if she'd be scared enough that you were going to tell your best friend or your daughter that she'd decide she'd better tell them first or if she'd just laugh the whole thing off, just say, "Boy, I must have been drunk, I can't believe I did that!"

And maybe eventually you'll look over at your wife, breathing heavily next to you, and for some reason you'll put your hand on the side of her face, for some reason you'll stroke her hair. Maybe for some reason you'll lean over and kiss her on the forehead and she'll moan and brush your hand away and, still breathing heavily, turn over and face the other way. Maybe you are even more of a coward but nothing is any better.

And yet, you remind yourself, the horn had been the best part of your bicycle. Your parents had given you the bike but you had bought the horn with money you'd made stripping paint off a house two blocks away.

And it is because words have no mass that they transmute so easily. It is because words are nothing more than abstractions that, if we repeat them over and over, they lose all meaning. It is because words are nothing more than abstractions that if we repeat them over and over, if we really look at them, they disappear. It is because they are nothing more than abstractions that if we repeat them over and over, day after day, to the same people, we realize words do not exist.

You are at dinner with a close friend. Two years ago he had called you and said, "I think this is really it." A couple of nights after that you had sat at a bar with a different, closer friend and both of you couldn't help laughing. What else was there to do? You made the usual bet. You gave them two years, Alex gave them six months. Now Alex has lost but you're not happy that either of you won. You really aren't.

When he called to tell you it was over at last, you invited him out to dinner and he eagerly jumped at the invitation. "I need to get out of this house," he said. Yet you feel no more sympathy for him than a doctor administering care to a patient, a patient who has done something stupid, a patient who left a lawn mower running while he fixed it "just so he could see where the problem was." You know what he needs and you give it to him but it requires no thought on your part. You go by the book, you have seen it many times before. For you this care is simply a matter of patiently going through the necessary steps. Then you know you will have done everything you can for him and only time will help with the rest of his convalescence.

The restaurant is very expensive, somewhere he could never afford. It is Italian, quiet, carved out of a cellar like a bomb shelter. There really are three-hundred-pound men in jogging suits and gold chains coming and going. But the food is the best Italian food in the country. It is a good place for diagnosis, a good place to ask him the questions he needs you to ask, a good place to nod your head and eat your risotto and not say very much.

He tells you how he never cheated on her (no, he never did, not to your knowledge — but what about that time six months ago when he called you and told you about that girl at his gym, the one who wore only Lycra shorts and a sports bra when she worked out, the one with the delicate nose stud, the one who would talk to him whenever she saw him, leave him openings to ask her out like telling him she had nothing to do that weekend, the one with the body, the one he said "couldn't have been more than nineteen or twenty," the one he had carefully avoided telling he was married, the one that was "driving him crazy," the one you told him you couldn't give him any advice about, the one about whom you said, "Do whatever you want. Life is short." — what about her?), how he never cheated on her, how he did more and more things just to please her, but that her insecurity got worse, not better. How at first he did things like train himself not to glance up over her shoulder when he caught shiny, healthy, blond hair out of the corner of his eye. How by the end if he was the first one home he would frantically mop the floor of the apartment, in a panic she would come home and scream at him that he had made it dirty because he knew she couldn't stand that.

He is embarrassed when he says that out loud, when he sees the look on your face. "It sounds ridiculous out loud, doesn't it? You can get used to anything, I guess, anything can become normal," he says. He takes a sip of the Château Lafite. "God that's good wine," he says.

He tells you about a sausage. About how she had thrown a sausage at him in the supermarket just a couple of weeks ago because it contained, among fifty other things, veal, and she hated veal, was against veal, and she had assumed he hadn't thought about that when he picked it out, hadn't thought about her when he picked it out, when in fact he had picked it out precisely because it was Greek and he knew she liked Greek delicacies. "She was always like that. She always assumed the worst about me," he says. "I don't know why."

But it was the dog that had finally done it. He tells you how they had gotten a dog recently, two months ago, how they had silently, mutually agreed that this would be a last-ditch attempt to save the relationship, that this would give them something to share. You don't tell him how even you know that was a bad idea, don't ask him why he hadn't known better, ask him what the hell he had been thinking it would give them to share besides a responsibility you could have told him neither of them wanted. He doesn't need to hear any of that right now. Instead you think, "Well, at least it wasn't a child." You think that because you've heard that one before too.

And so he goes on to tell you what you already know. How when they both got home from work neither of them wanted to walk that damn dog. How they both felt their own exhaustion was the more valid. How they would get into screaming matches every single night over who should be taking the ten minutes it took to take the dog downstairs and around the block. How they would end up calculating on paper who had done more walks. How sometimes, out of stubbornness, they would both sit there ignoring each other, ignoring the whining dog, until the dog went and peed in a corner which would, of course, start a whole new round of accusations.

Dessert arrives. It is especially good, superb. He loves it. "God, I've never had zabliogne like this!" he says, "It's like . . . like . . . like . . ." He is a writer, your friend.

"Like really good zabliogne?" you say.

He laughs. "Yes," he says, "like that."

And then afterwards he says "I'm not sure I want to go" and you say "Fine, I don't want to go if you don't want to go" and he says "Well I'll go if you want to go, don't not go because you think I don't want to go" and you say "I'm not going to go if you don't want to go, nine times out of ten it's the best thing but it doesn't work for everyone, there is some risk — Felix — you know Felix right? — when Felix got divorced it only made him angry to be there" and he says at last "OK, fine, let's go — but only for an hour or something and I'm not sure I want a dance or anything."

And then he sits there quietly for the rest of the ride, looking out the window. And so for the rest of the ride you wonder if she took the wedding presents with her when she left, you wonder if you will ever see her again, this woman you welcomed into your own life as well, this woman you made an effort to be friendly with even though she was a pain in the ass, even though she didn't try to be friendly with you, even though you knew — yes, knew — that she'd be gone sooner or later, even though she told your friend she didn't like his friends, that he spent too much time with them, even though your friend began spending less and less time with you because of her, alienated himself from you and his other friends, although you were going to be the one here, two years later, taking him out to dinner and holding his hand now they've finally realized for themselves what you could have told them two years ago when you first saw him so deliberately not check out a high school girl that had always been his type. This woman you welcomed into your life because your friend said he was in love with her.

And so what if you like her? So what if she's nice and makes an effort to get along with you, begins calling you up and telling you what your friends are doing, where everyone will be going that evening (a place she chose, a place none of you like in particular, a place that doesn't have particularly good food or beautiful girls but that will do because none of that really matters as along as everyone is there together, as long as going there means your friend, her significant other, can still be included), begins saying things like, "You know it's so-and-so's birthday next week — we really have to do something for him" when you've been doing something for so-and-so's birthday since she was in junior high. So what. Then you simply have to choose when they separate. And while you will always choose your friend, every now and then you will want to call that girl and see if she wants to come to the party you're having because she was really good company, she was fun to have around, and then you will be a little mad at your friend for fucking her in the first place instead of just staying friends with her. But you would never say any of this because all of this is just a minor irritation after all, a thought you would have while being driven across town, nothing more, because you know that compared to what your friend felt and is feeling, compared to what she felt and is feeling, all of this is trivial.

And so you are in a strip club again. You can't seem to get away from them. All over the world you find yourself in them. But this time it is not business or pleasure. It is therapy.

When you arrive there is already a bachelor party there. Young guys, large, probably recently out of college where they all lived in the same fraternity. As some more of them filter in behind you, they are greeted loudly, shout things like "Dozer!" and "BJ!" and "Bitch!" They hug. And when they sit down, they stay away from the seats around the edge of the stage where they would each be required to give every dancer a dollar. It is easy to pick the bachelor out from the others as you walk by. While his friends catch up with each other, while the ones now from New York talk to the ones now from San Francisco, while they do that, he just looks at the girls and sips the beers his friends buy him.

And as you walk past, on the way to the VIP room, away from the rabble, you aren't sure if your friend even notices them. Like the bachelor, he too is absorbed by the girls. Although his face carries a different kind of desperation. His face is more hungry than wistful, the bachelor's more wistful than hungry. And noticing this you can't help wondering how soon the bachelor will be back here with your friend's look, how soon he will be looking for a girl that will be his first and not his last.

The only qualification for the VIP room is the extra cover charge. You pay it for both of you. What you are paying for, what makes this an area for very important men, is that inside you can get a friction dance rather than a lap dance. For a friction dance, a completely naked girl straddles you, puts her arms around your neck, and gyrates her pelvis on top of your crotch. While she does this she may lean her torso back so you can see exactly how perfect her stomach is or she may sit upright and press your face into her breast implants or she may hunch over, touch her forehead to yours, and look into your eyes. A dance like this costs twice as much as a lap dance during which the girl is only topless and keeps one foot on the floor at all times. This is the only club in the entire Northeast to offer friction dances and just for this, on special occasions, groups of men come here from up to three hundred miles away.

When you enter, the open space of the VIP room proper is straight ahead, but on either side of you there are entrances to two dark corridors that stretch so far away their ends are lost in a dim, sweaty haze. Down these corridors are single rows of plush leather chairs. Sunken into many of the chairs are men. Climbing on top of the men, writhing slowly, in various states of undress, are women. Corridors, areas, like this always remind you of nothing so much as a painting of Hell you own, a painting of Hell you bought because it reminded you of corridors, areas, like this.

Somehow, when you sit down, the girls immediately smell blood. Some of them circle for a minute or two, wander past your table as if looking nearby for someone specific but being sure to turn around facing towards your table rather than away. You are always amazed by their ability to pick out the men willing and able to spend money from the men who just paid the extra cover to buy one beer and nurse it for two hours while they watch the all-nude stage show. There is a well-dressed man quite near you yet the girls completely ignore him and home in on you even though you are wearing blue jeans and a T-shirt and a baseball cap. They somehow even manage to distinguish you from your friend because when at last one of them comes and asks if she can sit at your table, she asks you, sits next to you, talks to you. You always compare it to that summer you worked in your father's jewelry store. By August you could tell the moment someone walked in whether or not they were going to buy something. But even then, even when it was you, you couldn't have said how you did it.

The girl who sits next to you and talks to you is far from the most beautiful girl in the place. It is always like that too. The girls that are not so pretty work harder, solicit. The men make a point of finding the beautiful girls. The beautiful girls are so much in demand they can even sometimes pick and choose who they dance for.

You do not look at her as she talks to you, about her night, about how hot it is in here. You are not rude but there is no reason to pay anything more than the most rudimentary attention to her. She is neither beautiful nor young. Your friend is eagerly looking at the stage where a truly stunning girl dances, a girl with extremely expensive implants, with a really convincing half-wig that makes it look like her hair would be three feet long if it wasn't gathered up into that fake ponytail on top of her head. Eventually the girl next to you gets up and goes away, says, "Well, let me know if you want a dance later."

This isn't a sleazy place, the chairs are leather, the floors are carpeted. The bouncers are enormous and would throw anyone out if they got too drunk. But that's not going to happen when even the cheapskates nursing their one beer still had at least fifty dollars to spend on looking at naked women. This place makes its money off the girls, not the liquor. But you are still able to order a bottle of good champagne, and you do so, tipping the waitress well. The men treat the waitresses and cigarette girls in these places terribly, order them around in ways they never would the dancers. The men want the dancers to think they're gentlemen. They don't care what the waitresses and cigarette girls think as long as they give them their drinks and their cigars. So they try all kinds of things with them they'd never try with the dancers, try to get them to sit in their laps, ask them to bend over more when they serve the drinks. With the dancers, the women they can pay to gyrate naked in their laps, they are often almost shy. And as if that weren't enough, the men frequently tip the servers badly too. Saving money for the dancers, they don't like to tip. You once saw a guy who had just spent six hundred dollars on dances and had a three-hundred-dollar bar tab not tip his waitress at all. Not a penny. So you tip yours well. You're a nice guy, thoughtful. And she appreciates it, is surprised, grateful, says, "Let me know if you need anything else, I'll be back in a minute to check on you."

The truly stunning girl is done dancing so, telling your friend you are going to the men's room, you intercept her as she comes offstage, ask her if she'd like to come and sit with you and your friend and have some champagne. She says she'll be right there. She is exactly what the doctor ordered.

When she arrives at your table and just sits down without a word, your friend is surprised. His eyes light up and he glances at you and smiles.

The three of you chat for a while. She says she has only recently started dancing again, that she was "doing something else" for a year. When you ask her what she was doing she laughs and says, "I was married." But he was too jealous, she tells you, even after they were married, even when she stopped dancing, he was too jealous. So they just got divorced and she had to go back to work. "You have to make money somehow," she says.

Eventually you send her and your friend off to one of the corridors. "Stay there as long as he likes," you tell her. She takes your friend's hand, leads him through the room. Sheepishly your friend goes off with her, his eyes at last daring to dart all over her body. Halfway across the room, she looks back at him and says something that makes him laugh. This is what he needed, a dancer with a lot of experience. When he has his confidence back he'll lose interest in dancers like that, in dancers that smile seductively when they're facing you but whose faces go blank as soon as they turn away. When he has his confidence back he'll want an inexperienced girl, one who isn't too jaded, who isn't so familiar with the physical motions, so practiced, that she doesn't have to make herself enjoy herself to give a good dance. But for now he needs someone who will think for him, who will remind him what he likes. You know that as much as it should be like riding a bicycle, it isn't. Every time you fall off you need someone to teach you how to do it again.

Almost as soon as they are gone, another girl asks if she can sit next to you. She is far from pretty, it looks like her nose may have once been broken, but she is young. Very young. "This is more like it," you think, this is exactly what you wanted to amuse yourself with while you wait for your friend. You say, "Of course . . . please . . . ," pull out a chair, offer her some champagne. She refuses, you can't understand why, but she clearly takes it as a good sign anyway. Her shoulders relax. You hadn't noticed how tense they were until she let them relax.

And she is relieved too when you begin to question her, she didn't know what she was supposed to say. And you are fascinated by her. Genuinely fascinated. You love her regional accent, the suggestion that she has not been exposed to very much. And when she tells you she is a freshman in college you are slightly more interested. Even though this doesn't surprise you, even though you suspected as much, hearing her actually make the claim still excites you a little more. Now you find yourself examining what parts of her flesh you can see outside her gown. It is very pale and very supple. Now you want to know what she looks like naked. Now you want to run the backs of your fingers over her exposed shoulders, over her neck. Now it is you who smells blood.

You ask her how long she's been dancing. She tells you this is only her third night ever and her first time here, dancing fully nude. The idea that she hasn't danced for many men before is even more exciting than her being a freshman and the idea that you might be the first man to pay her to dance completely naked is even more exciting than that. You wonder if she would tremble at all as she danced for you, if her skin would shiver slightly or break out in a cold sweat when you caressed it. You wonder if she would be able to look into your eyes for very long even if you told her to.

"Are you nervous?" you ask.

"A little," she says. "But I guess it's only a teensy-weensy bit more fabric I have to take off."

You smile at this. You hadn't thought of it that way.

She points out a girl dancing on the stage, dancing very professionally. "My friend brought me in here — she says you make a lot more money here."

"Is she a freshman too?" you ask. Her friend is beautiful.

"Yup," she says.

Now you wonder if her friend's breasts are actually real. They seem too perfect for that but you have to wonder where she could have gotten the money for that good a job. They must be real you decide. And then you wonder how an eighteen-year-old girl learned to dance like that.

You turn back to the girl at your table. "Are you sure you wouldn't like a drink?" you ask.

She thinks for a minute, looking off into the distance, her eyes shifting around, and then, as something occurs to her, she smiles, turns her head to you, looks at you, and says, "OK, I'll have a Shirley Temple."

A Shirley Temple! You don't show it, at least you think you don't show it, but you are very amused. That's why she didn't want any champagne — she isn't old enough to drink and she doesn't know if she can on this first night in this new club, doesn't want to take the chance of blowing this opportunity, of embarrassing her friend who vouched for her or, even worse, getting her in trouble.

With a grin you order the girl a Shirley Temple from the waitress. She is very surprised, repeats it back to you as a question. You nod. She shrugs, brings the drink. The girl sips it, leaving a ring of lipstick around the straw.

And ordering this drink for this girl has now made you crazy for her. You love that you are sitting there with a girl who still likes to drink Shirley Temples but that you could pay to press her naked pussy against you at any moment you chose.

And you realize that right here, right now, in this case, this has nothing to do with anything other than being delighted with the idea you could be a corrupter. That you could just reach out and pluck something from the sky and drag it down. That you could snatch this perfect thing up and watch it wilt in your hand. Yet not, like a Mongol, taking pleasure in the destruction for its own sake (as you sometimes think you would enjoy doing in your darkest, most angry moments). But instead taking pleasure in the destruction because the act that causes it also happens to be an act that makes you feel good. As if the actual act of cutting flowers to decorate your house was just as pleasurable as looking at them once the fresh-cut blossoms were in place. You are delighted by the idea that if you were to make this girl dance for you, while the act was giving you pleasure, it would be consuming something in her that could never return. As if on a cold, cold night not only the warmth and dance of the fire gave you pleasure, but also the fact that the wood must be burned to produce the fire. For some reason, the fact that the thing is used up in the process, the idea that no one else can ever have exactly what you had, is tremendously exciting. It is precisely the same feeling you have had whenever you and you alone have consumed a unique bottle of precious wine. Anyone can understand that, can't they? That this makes you feel special, set apart from all other men even if in only a very small way?

And as you recognize this, you understand why when you have shared a girl like this with one or even two of your closest friends, it has brought you even closer together, because you have shared a pleasurable experience that no one else has ever had or can ever have again.

Then you have a wonderful idea. You could get her and her friend to dance together for you. You could get these two eighteen-year-old, Shirley Temple–drinking freshmen to press their bodies together, to grind their pussies on each other's thighs as they danced, to kiss. That would be even more depraved, even more degrading, and thus even more destructive. That would leave even less behind for those who came after you.

And that is exactly what you do. You have her call her friend over to the table and you tell them what you want. At first they are reluctant, they've never done anything like that before, which is of course exactly what you want. But it turns out, like almost everything in your experience, to be only a question of money. You agree to pay them double the normal rate each to dance for you for an hour. But they still have to check with a manager, they are delightfully ignorant of the club's policy regarding something like this. The girl you sent your friend off with wouldn't have been. Naturally the management has no problem with it.

As you make your way back into the depths of the corridor you pass your friend but he doesn't even see you. He is dead to the world, anesthetized.

When they first start dancing, they are a little awkward, they look at each other more than they look at you, a little embarrassed by each other's flesh, suddenly aware of the nakedness they only recently shared together in the dressing room without a second thought. It is the girl who has been dancing longer who finally takes the lead, who at last slips one thigh between her friend's legs and pulls her close, crushes their breasts together. And with that, as if they had finally taken the dive into a pool they knew was cold, they are suddenly relaxed. They begin to look at you more than each other as they rub their bodies together, slide up and down each other. And as the hour progresses you are pleased to see that towards the end the situation has reversed again, that towards the end the girls are paying so much attention to each other's bodies, are so involved in their long, open-mouthed kisses, that they have stopped looking at you altogether. Towards the end you note with satisfaction that when one's thigh rubs between the other's legs, it comes out glistening.

When you went down the corridor, they had looked a little sick, as if they were getting on a roller coaster they weren't sure they wanted to ride, they weren't even holding hands. But now when you pay them, when you count out the hundred-dollar bills, when you give them 30 percent extra for a job well done, they look flushed, happy, as if they're glad they did it after all. They stand next to each other, naked, with their arms still around each other's waists. They only stop touching each other to count their money.

While you wait for them to count it, before they thank you and smile at you and tell you they hope you'll come back (which you won't – not for them – they have nothing to offer you now), before they put their clothes back on, you think about how if either of these girls moved in with you and asked you for a dog, you would never have the problems your friend had. If one of these girls lived with you and asked you for a dog and you agreed, from the beginning you would no more assume she would share responsibility for the animal than you would a six-year-old. If she asked you for a dog, you would know what you were getting into.

Your friend is done too and you leave. Outside, breathing the fresh night air in deep, he says, "God I feel great! I don't know – like I've had something painful removed, like something heavy is gone. I mean, I know I'll feel worse in the morning, I know that, but it won't be as bad as this morning I don't think. It's like she reminded me there really are other things out there."

As you both get in your limo he adds, "She'd be furious if she knew I'd been here tonight."

"Why?" you ask. "She left you, you're through, what business is it of hers?"

He nods. Looks out the window, taps the tinted glass with the index finger of one hand. It makes a little tinking sound. "She'd still be furious," he says. Then he looks at you and adds, "Especially at you. Boy, would she be pissed at you."

"I know," you say. "I know." Then, "What happened to the dog?"

And what if we don't do any of this? What if we don't have the opportunity or the time or do have too much integrity to lie to our wives or too much self-control to indulge ourselves at another's expense, whether hers or her parents'? What then?

Then we go out and buy ourselves a motorcycle. We buy a black leather jacket to go with it. Then we sell all our antiques and buy expensive furniture made by some Finnish designer, start listening to music that is more popular (with who?) than the music we used to listen to but is still six months out of date. Then we start collecting expensive comic books. Then we make fools of ourselves anyway but with nothing to show for it. Certainly nothing that could make other men look at you with lasting envy, that could make them think about you, a stranger, later that day or week and think "that lucky bastard," that could make them lash out at their wife or girlfriend later that day over something they would otherwise have been patient about. Certainly nothing that could make older women look at you, a stranger, with rage rather than amusement or pity. Certainly nothing about which you could say with tremendous satisfaction, "Laugh all you want, perhaps I am making a fool of myself. Perhaps this is, for some reason, undignified, beneath me. Perhaps, for some reason I should know better. But it's worth it. It's worth it because when I go home tonight, I get to fuck her as much as I want, this girl, this fast, young thing."

You will be standing on the shoreline of a river where you played as a child, drank as a teenager. You will stand there with your daughter and stare out over the water, over at the other side. She will insist on lipstick and on earrings but will still hold your hand when it's cold, sometimes even when it isn't.

"Daaaad," she will whine, "what're we doing here? It's cold."

"I don't understand," you will say, "there used to be a factory over there across the river. A run-down abandoned factory. You could look at it for hours. It had all kinds of machines running into it and coming out of it. No one ever knew what it did — but that was why it used to be so fascinating. This used to be a really cool spot to just hang out."

"Dad," she will say with a withering look, a look you will not catch as you look out over the water at the new yacht club on the other side, "Dad, nobody says 'hang out' anymore . . . and nobody cares about how things used to be."

When did the embassy succeed with us? When did we take up our shields in spite of our rage?

And when did that which was offered disfigure us? How does glory make us rot? How does something we cannot touch, or see, or even define, do so much damage, make us so miserable?

How did we get so ugly?

I would like to thank Mark Rudman, Loren Fishman, and my editor, Judy Clain. Without them, this never would have happened. Dan Degnan, Jim Higdon, James Tierney, Carole Maso, Meredith Steinbach, and Bob Coover were also tremendously helpful. Claire Smith and Sarah Burnes have my gratitude for their patience in answering all my questions, while Steve Lamont has it for his unwavering eye. Nick Mills and Edward Baron Turk should know they have always been inspirations to me. Finally I would, of course, like to thank Alfred and Janice for their support and belief through all the years.

Although the rules for punctuation, capitalization, and grammar are well established, in this book I have chosen to experiment with their limitations. For example, punctuation in *girls* reflects narrative rhythm rather than grammatical convention, while capitalization frequently reflects the tone of a word rather than the ordinary mechanics of typography. Any perceived "errors" along these lines are entirely intentional.

Nic Kelman was a Burchard Scholar at MIT, where he studied brain and cognitive sciences as an undergraduate. After spending a few years working in independent film, he attended Brown University on a full fellowship for his MFA in creative writing, where he was awarded the James Assatly prize for graduate fiction. He now writes and teaches in New York City, where he lives with his girlfriend of thirteen years and his dog.